THE WINEMAKER'S DINNER
Dessert

Dr. Ivan Rusilko

OMNIFIC PUBLISHING
DALLAS

Omnific Publishing
10000 North Central Expressway, Dallas, TX 75231
www.omnificpublishing.com

First Omnific eBook edition, April 2013
First Omnific trade paperback edition, April 2013

The characters and events in this book are fictitious.
Any similarity to real persons, living or dead,
is coincidental and not intended by the author.

Library of Congress Cataloguing-in-Publication Data

Rusilko, Dr. Ivan.
    The Winemaker's Dinner: Dessert / Dr. Ivan Rusilko – 1st ed.
    ISBN: 978-1-623420-31-4
    1. Contemporary Romance — Fiction. 2. Erotica — Fiction.
    3. Miami — Fiction. 4. Celebrity Chef — Fiction. I. Title

10 9 8 7 6 5 4 3 2 1

Cover Design by Micha Stone and Amy Brokaw
Interior Book Design by Coreen Montagna
Photography by John Conroy (www.johnconroy.com)
Cover models: Dr. Ivan Rusilko and Adrienne Martinez

Printed in the United States of America

To the one girl I will love forever. ;)

CHAPTER 1
"Hotel California"

"Oh! Fuck, yes!"

The sound of utter ecstasy rebounded off the dimly lit hotel room walls and ricocheted into the cool Miami Beach winter's night. The ocean breeze carried the faint but sweet smell of burning *colitas* through an open window, providing Ivan momentary relief from the heat radiating between his torso and the body bent over the bed in front of him.

"You like that." It wasn't a question but a command. His voice was barely more than a growl, resonating with power and dripping with control. His thrusts increased, and he pounded into her hard—maybe even harder than he should have—but she loved it. The crazed, glassy-eyed look on her face told him as much.

"Ah, fuck!" was the only response she had for him as she tossed her jet black hair away from her face and across her back, practically begging his inner beast to pull it.

A mirror on the wall opposite the bed reflected the erotic scene playing out in front of them, one of dominance and submission, power and control. Ivan grinned into the mirror as he saw a smile sweep across her lips. She looked through the mirror and directly into his eyes, watching him watch her get off. She raked her hands down the sheets and clenched the white linen between her fingers as he took her from behind, her gaze transfixed on the man in the mirror.

Ivan couldn't help but revel in the reflected show he was enjoying. He reached forward and grabbed a fist full of hair, pulling her head back and once again exerting his dominance over her and her body. Harder and harder he fucked her without mercy. All she could do—all he would allow her to do—was brace herself against the bed and succumb to his domination. She moaned as he held her firm, one hand gripping her ass and the other her hair.

Faster and harder he forced himself into her as her panting morphed into a string of mangled profanity, further fueling his lust. Her body bounded back and forth, and she screamed in pleasure as the figure in the mirror dug his fingers into her hips, fucking her like a madman.

Finally he felt her tremble under his control. He quickened his pace and wielded his power with forceful upward strokes that lifted her feet off the floor. Seeming to want all he could give, she rose up on her tiptoes to give him even more access, which he greedily took. His body began to splinter in an all-too-familiar way, and he started down the inevitable path to orgasm. His cock firmed and his spine loosened, readying his body for release. He tightened his grip on her hair, jerking her head farther back as he reached around and teased her swollen clit with hard, meaningful strokes. Each one drove her toward frenzy, and she began to scream when her body convulsed in pleasure. She tightened around his cock like a vice.

Ivan felt her body climax, but that didn't stop him. Needing his fix, he drove himself back into her. He released her hair and flipped her onto her back as if she was weightless, all the while marveling at her naked form: perfect, delicate, and properly fucked. His mind released a rush of endorphins—a reward for making her come—but there was another need to satisfy. His addiction remained unfed. The smell of sex engulfed him, and without a word he grabbed her legs and pulled her to the edge of the bed, bringing the backs of her knees to rest on his shoulders. His hands wrapped around the back of her neck, and he pressed his forearms against her shoulders, leveraging himself against her body and deepening his thrusts. Ivan began to invade her with every inch he had, making his intentions clear: he wanted, no, he *needed* to come.

Every inward stroke brought him closer and closer to a nirvana he longed for, but it was in the shimmer of her green eyes and the blackness of her hair that he found what he was looking for. His spine tingled and his toes flexed against the wooden floor as his own release began to overcome him.

"Harder!" she commanded.

The sound of flesh on flesh and panting screams filled the room, and Ivan, now the obedient one, pushed harder, driving himself toward his sexual heaven and relishing the sound of her passion. With a final thrust he plunged inside her, finally achieving the orgasmic bliss he craved. A rush of warmth ran through his lower back and his dick convulsed. His arms squeezed her thighs and his hands cupped the back of her neck as a final spasm rocketed through his body.

Without warning, a warm and gentle hand ran up the back of his thigh and across his ass, piercing through his sexual oblivion. His breath was still uneven and his cock still buried in the girl he'd just finished fucking as he turned to acknowledge another expectant lady standing next to him. She was naked.

The invitation for a second go 'round with an even more adventurous third party and the annoying feeling of the restriction of a condom was all it took to strip away the last of Ivan's sexual haze and snap his mind back to a reality that wasn't at all what he wanted. His now-clear vision exposed the situation around him for what it was. The locks of ebony hair that cascaded across her shoulders were not ebony at all, but a dirty shade of blond, and the shimmering green eyes that he thought had mesmerized him morphed into a pool of ordinary brown. The legs he'd caressed didn't belong to the dark-haired, green-eyed Colorado beauty who had touched his soul, but instead to a blond-haired, brown-eyed Miami Beach land shark who did little more than tickle his dick.

"Mind if I join you?" the woman beside him asked, squeezing his ass as she stroked the blonde's inner thigh. "I want a taste."

Remorse filled the base of Ivan's skull, and he knew no amount of faceless sex would ever fill the void that lingered in his chest. Swallowing hard, he replied, "Why don't the two of you start without me?"

Ms. Waiting-To-Be-Fucked smiled and nodded. She slid her hands around Ivan's waist and eased him out of the other girl's body. The women erupted into a fit of giggles as Ms. Freshly-Fucked captured her friend by the shoulders and tossed her onto the bed. There she straddled her legs while she cooed and kissed the nape of her neck.

Falling back onto a chair, Ivan took a minute to marvel at the sight unfolding in front of him. His dick did more than marvel as blood rushed into it, causing it to grow hard and wanting again.

"Do you like this?"

Ms. Freshly-Fucked's voice cut through him like a rusty knife, reminding him of his weakness for the flesh. Staring at them with a hard cock and mindless gaze, he simply nodded and smiled as they began to work each other over. The sight of them, naked, kissing, and touching while they beckoned for him to join, should have felt like winning the sexual lottery. Instead, it felt as if poisonous toxins were seeping into his body through every pore. Even two girls burning with need for him wasn't enough morphine to medicate the hell he'd been living in the past six months—six long and painful months since his baby girl walked out of his life.

The loneliness that engulfed him every day was now his companion. Jaden was gone forever, never to lie by his side again. The random sexual conquests that had become his drug of choice since she'd betrayed him were merely Band-Aids to his hemorrhaging heart. But they were his only salve against the complete and utter devastation Jaden had left in her wake. Ivan hated it, but he couldn't avoid it. Jaden's indiscretions had made him a prisoner of his own device.

Life was nothing more than a faded black-and-white movie now, and the occasional thirty minutes of sex, endorphins, and vivid imagination were his sole glimpses of the once-familiar rainbow palette of colors that had painted his mornings and brightened the nights lost in her gaze. But these glimpses were just a mirage. It was life's dick tease, nothing more than a lie to numb his mind and soothe the pain that tortured his soul.

"Come join us?" the girls asked in unison.

Their breasts ground together as they explored each other's bodies, inside and out. It was a sexual feast begging to be eaten, figuratively and literally. Two gorgeous, sexual creatures taunted him with sweet sins of the flesh, but try as he might, Ivan couldn't bring himself to say yes. It didn't feel right. It never did. He'd gotten his fix for the night, and even though they were stunning, something was missing. It wasn't *her*. It would never be *her*.

Ivan cleared his throat and closed his eyes, blocking out the tempting scene on the bed before him. "I would love to, but I have to get up early tomorrow. I have patients to see."

"Tomorrow's Saturday," one of them moaned through building ecstasy. "You work on the weekend?"

Ivan knew it didn't matter what tale he told. So he'd been caught in a careless and quick lie. So what? Indifferent to the girls' feelings or the web of lies he was spinning, he bent over to pull on his pants and shirt. "Yeah, concierge medicine," he finally said. "I work when I have to."

"That's too bad," Ms. Freshly-Fucked moaned, continuing to bring her friend to climax.

It occurred to him that she seemed rather indifferent about whether he stayed and participated, left, or just stood beside the bed and took in the show.

Quickening her pace, she looked up at him, momentarily taking her attention away from the body writhing beneath her. "Lock the door on your way out, will you?"

"Have fun, ladies." Ivan chuckled and felt his dick twitch, asking him one last time if he was serious about leaving. He scolded himself for falling prey to the weakness within him, but he had nowhere to turn but an endless string of warm bodies that kept him sated for thirty minutes a night. This heaven was his hell.

He slipped his shoes on and paused to say a final goodbye, but what was the point? They'd already dismissed him and were on about their business of fucking each other. He breathed out a soft laugh and headed for the door, sport jacket in hand. Rather than mentally high fiving such a sexual conquest, Ivan couldn't shake the feeling that he was doing some unknown injustice to himself and a relationship that no longer existed.

As the door creaked open and he stepped into the hallway, the sounds of a white-hot female orgasm echoed after him, taunting him. But what was left of his conscience urged him toward the elevators. After pressing the call button, he ran his hand along the scruff of a beard on his jaw, trying to block out the images of the black-haired, green-eyed goddess that haunted him before, during, and after each and every deviant encounter.

The elevator arrived, and he quickly stepped in. A feeling of familiar numbness washed over him as the doors slid shut, leaving him alone with his thoughts in a small metal box. The images that raced through his mind chased away all lingering effects of his sexual fix, and he knew it would soon be forgotten, just as he'd forgotten all the others. The elevator descended and so did Ivan, once again plunged into his own personal hell.

"Fuck," he grumbled, shaking his head and trying to clear it of all thought. The doors of the elevator opened, and forcing one foot in front of the other, Ivan strolled out through the lobby and into the night—alone and still searching for that place he was before.

CHAPTER 2

"Time to Move On"

"So, do you have any big plans for the next few months?" Kevin peered at Jaden across his oversized desk.

This was their final wrap-up meeting of the season. They'd had strategy sessions and critiques already, so this one was really just a formality—and a formality Jaden was wondering why she had to bother with. It was her last remaining obstacle before she and the rest of the *One Hot Kitchen* crew would be released on a two-month hiatus, and she wouldn't see Kevin until shooting for the next season commenced. Jaden smoothed her hands over the thin cotton fabric of her green sundress, forced her lips into a smile, and looked at him with as much enthusiasm as she could gather. Though her eyes were the same emerald green they'd always been, she now saw things so differently than when she'd first arrived in L.A. and sat in this exact spot, talking to the same man. No matter how hard she tried, there was no way she could be that stars-in-her-eyes-excited girl Kevin had welcomed more than a year ago. *A whole year. Has it really been that long?*

"I'm planning on heading back to Miami for a while. I'll visit friends and unplug for a bit." Even as the words rolled out of her mouth, a stab of pain flashed through her mind at the thought of crossing paths with the man she'd singlehandedly broken. Images of Ivan's face the last time she saw him filled her head and replayed in slow motion. It was a face filled with sorrow, confusion, and complete disappointment.

Kevin looked at her for a moment, almost as if he sympathized with her situation. But he'd been careful to keep their relationship strictly professional lately, and in an instant it was back to business as usual for the head of the network. "That sounds great," he said cheerily. "A little sun and fun will have you looking good as new. Plus, it'll give you time to prepare for next season. Miami has some great food and wine festivals, so I'll be sure to set up some appearances for you, maybe even a hosting job or two. You need to maximize your time as much as you can during the off-season and come back here ready to go at it. You've got some big shoes to fill now that you're flying solo again."

Big shoes? Looking as good as new? Ugh. Clearly Kevin had different feelings about Damian Gris's departure—and perhaps about her—than she did. *I'm the one that made this show, and I'm the reason there's still a show to come back to! The fucking nerve of him.* He seemed to have rewritten history and no longer remembered the train wreck the show had been by the end of the season. Whatever on-camera chemistry she and Damian had managed to fake for a while had pretty much unraveled after she punched him. And though she'd been careful to be nothing but cordial and professional on the set, Damian had refused to play ball. A show just doesn't work when one host doesn't really know much about cooking and is focused only on sabotaging the other.

Kevin was lucky she was coming back at all. *One Hot Kitchen* just wasn't that much fun anymore, and it had cost her more than she could ever afford. It did amuse her a little that Kevin's solution to the problem had been giving Damian his own show, *What A Man Wants.* She was thankful not to have to deal with that son of a bitch messing around in her kitchen any more, but he was still associated with the network, and now they'd be competing for time slots. But there was no point in saying any of this right now, so she just sighed.

"Yes, I'm looking forward to some time off to clear my head," Jaden said. "But I'm sure if you wanted to plan an appearance or two for me while I'm in Miami it would be beneficial for the show." *Just don't get too carried away,* she added silently. *I really do need a break.*

"I just want you to be on your game next season. I anticipate that we'll surpass last season's numbers, and who better to promote the show than our shining star? I expect you'll attend whatever events I can arrange, especially since you're still under contract."

With that, the elephant in the room flexed its muscles. Kevin had pulled the ace of spades from his sleeve.

"I know everything that happened between you and Ivan must've been very difficult, but this is a business and—"

"Kevin, I get it," Jaden said, cutting him off. There was certainly no need to go *there*.

"Okay, good. I just wanted to be clear. When next season starts, I expect you back in L.A. with a clear mind and ready to go."

Jaden couldn't help but wonder if Damian had also received this sort of "Professionalism 101" pep talk. Probably not, though he'd shown he needed it. But why was she even thinking about him? At the root of things, she'd created this mess. She'd brought her personal life into *One Hot Kitchen*, and as much as she might resent Kevin's insinuations, she'd opened the door for this all by herself.

She just needed some time to get past it, to recharge, and frankly, that time couldn't come soon enough. She managed a nod and a smile. "Is that it?"

Kevin looked back at her as if he might say something else, but then nodded.

"Great. Thank you." In one motion she was on her feet and heading for the door.

"I'll be in touch!" he called as the door closed behind her.

Propelled by a growing desire to be out of L.A., Jaden crossed the vast expanse of the lot and entered the building that housed the set. On the way to her dressing room, she passed a swarm of crew members transforming the set of *One Hot Kitchen* into whatever show would take its place for the next few months.

"Jaden! *Jaden!*"

Her name echoed down the hall in time to the sound of heels clicking against a tiled floor, and she knew instantly who was calling.

"I'm glad I caught you before you left."

Jaden turned to face Stacey, dressed in her typical designer cougar attire. "What's up?"

"Just wanted to say goodbye before you left. What are your plans while the show is on hiatus?"

"I'm going to Miami to spend some time with friends and maybe even do some cooking at Bianca for fun. Plus, I think Kevin has a few events he wants me to attend while I'm there."

"You're going to Miami?" Stacey sounded surprised, as if Miami were the last place she expected Jaden to go. "Are you going to see Ivan? That boy hasn't returned any of my calls."

Me neither, Jaden thought, remembering the countless phone calls, text messages, and emails that all remained unanswered. Her heart sank all over again as she pictured her last contact with Ivan: she'd been screaming at the top of her lungs about sleeping with another man.

Did Ivan even know that she'd been mistaken? That nothing had happened with Damian that terrible night? Surely he must—she'd told him over and over in her unanswered correspondence. But had he even read her messages? Probably not. Or else he had and that detail didn't matter. Either way, Jaden felt rotten to the core.

"No, I haven't talked to him," she told Stacey. She looked at the floor. "I doubt I'll be seeing him."

Mercifully, Stacey changed the subject. "Oh, okay, well, I'm sure you'll have fun visiting with your old friends. Try to recharge while you're there, okay? Relax and enjoy the weather."

"I'll do my best."

"I'll see you in two months, Jaden. Take care."

"Thanks, Stacey. You too." She watched Stacey click her way on down the hall and realized she'd seemed genuine. How strange to be at odds with Kevin but perfectly understood by her over-the-top former nemesis.

After collecting the last of her personal items from the dressing room and saying a surprisingly teary farewell to Kat, she made her way outside to the cab she'd called for earlier. Adam was on vacation with his family, and she wouldn't have the opportunity to see him before she left for Miami. Of course today she could've used one of his front seat/backseat therapy sessions, but it would have to wait.

She slipped into the back of the black and gold cab and gave the driver her address, then shifted her attention to the passing scenery as the cab weaved through the heavy L.A. traffic. Tom Petty sang on the radio about moving on, and though she tried to keep her mind blank, she couldn't help but rethink her upcoming trip to Miami. Was it the best idea? If she ever had any hopes of getting over Ivan, Miami was probably the last place she needed to be. She would likely run in to him at some point. The thought of it terrified her, but nevertheless, a sliver of excitement crept up her spine, along with the word that defines the most distant of hopes: *maybe*.

Maybe she would run into him. Maybe he would run into her. Maybe they'd run into each other. Maybe he had forgiven her. Maybe he was finally ready to talk. Maybe he wanted to see her. And maybe, just maybe, they could work it all out somehow. The world was at her fingertips, if she could just get herself together and prevent it from slipping away. Perhaps this trip was her chance to mend two broken hearts.

As the cab pulled up to her house, she handed the driver some money and ran to the front door of her apartment. She was once again ready to go.

CHAPTER 3

"Grace is Gone"

*I*t used to be the tranquil sounds of thunder and soft rain drifting through the speakers of his stereo that lulled him to sleep, but like everything else in the past six months, that too had changed. Now the steady and monotonous tick of a metronome provided the only possible respite for a mind that raced a million miles a minute and often refused to shut down. Lying in bed, Ivan squeezed his eyes shut against the far off city lights that glowed through the blinds of his new apartment. He couldn't help but think how much *she* would love the view from here. Sure, the rent was way more expensive at this end of the island, but the old place had constantly dredged up unwanted memories. Plus, he was at the helm of his own business — his own medical enterprise — now, and he needed to look the part. He deserved to enjoy what his hard work had made possible.

Exhausted, Ivan exhaled, ready to forfeit any hopes of a full night's sleep. He blinked his eyes open, and even though he knew it was some ungodly hour, he snuck a look at the clock on his phone. "Two thirty? Damn it." He pulled back the comforter and sat up, letting his legs dangle over the side of the bed. "What now?"

He weighed his options. Wine was the first thing that came to mind. Without another thought, he sprang from the bed, phone in hand, and headed to the kitchen. He pressed the button at the bottom of the screen and used its light to navigate his way through the darkened and still not entirely familiar apartment.

Focused on the refrigerator, he rounded the corner and locked his eyes on it, bathed in the warm glow of an overhead spotlight. It held the only known prescription for his newest post-breakup stress disorder: insomnia. Goose bumps rose on his forearms, reminding him that the AC was cranked up full blast, and he was standing in the middle of the kitchen wearing nothing more than a pair of white Calvin Klein's. He swung the fridge door open and a wave of even cooler air washed over him as he squinted against the bright interior lights and cursed again.

Ivan tucked his phone into the waistband of his boxer briefs and reached for a bottle of his good old standby, Miss Molly, then shut the door against the arctic chill prickling his skin. As his eyes once again adjusted to the darkness, he reached for a wineglass on the nearby rack and made a beeline to the balcony. As he crossed the room to the patio's sliding glass doors, the size of the apartment made him feel even more alone. Many of his friends would've given anything to have this much square footage, but there was nothing familiar or comforting about his new apartment. Everything was new and pristine—even the bed he'd once shared with her was gone. The interior designer had assured him that everything was chic and top of the line, but it didn't feel like home. Nowhere had felt like home since he'd left her sitting in the parking lot of The Bath Club six months ago.

As the patio door slid open, he welcomed the warm air that washed over his body. He stumbled to the oversized chair in the corner of the patio, fumbling with the cork. He tossed aside the twisted wire, took aim, and popped the cork into the blackness of the night from twenty stories up. The unmistakable sound it created resonated for what sounded like miles, traveling down to the marina and off toward the city. He listened intently as he tipped the bottle to the glass and carbonation escaped the ruby red elixir—a wonderful red shiraz. Its fizzing was the only thing that seemed familiar and at all comforting this night.

Ivan lounged back in the chair and crossed his right leg over his left, alone with himself, his thoughts, and a full glass of Miss Molly. In time, one glass turned into two, and his thoughts shifted from "Where am I going?" to "What have I become?" He looked over his shoulder and back through the glass sliding doors at his surroundings: the fine art that hung from the walls, the framed achievements that had taken him years to acquire, and the family photos that reminded him he was not truly alone. He congratulated himself for making it, for becoming a successful business man. The business he'd worked so hard to build, with nearly singular focus, was thriving. He should be enjoying the spoils of his effort now, he reminded himself again, but every day he struggled with the worry that nothing lasts forever. Even when everything seems fantastic…sometimes it's not. He fought to convince himself that not everything was disposable. He was in charge of his career, even if his personal life was in ruins.

But the upgraded ocean view and doubled square footage he now basked in was nothing more than a cover up for his failed love life. Ivan had been so hell-bent on making drastic changes since *that night* that he'd even traded his old girl, Betty, for a sleek new lady, Candy. Sure, she drove like a dream, and the new car symbolized his success, but the Mercedes SLS just didn't fill him with the same joy Betty had. Nothing in his life seemed the same anymore, and a big part of him wondered if it ever would. Without Jaden, all the success and achievements he'd worked so hard to be able to enjoy had created nothing more than a really beautiful, but really lonely, tomb.

The next glass of wine went down smoothly, but it also conjured remembrances of what was, what could have been, and what should have been. Right now, she would've been neck deep in planning their future and their happily ever after. They would've talked of buying a house, having kids, and imagined their life together. It seemed Miss Molly had released the floodgates on all the memories that plagued him — even if they were memories of things that never were.

A part of him still felt a little unsettled by the fact that he hadn't seen or spoken to her since the night his life fell apart. Not a day went by that she didn't email, text, or phone him, but all her messages remained unopened, unread, and unanswered. Ivan knew deep down that he couldn't stomach any excuse she'd try to give — not then and not now. *Fuck that*, he thought and poured another glass of red. *She still works with the fucker!*

On the rare occasion that he watched TV, he skipped the station that hosted *One Hot Kitchen*, but once or twice when channel surfing, he'd caught a flash of her and that dickhead Damian playing it up for the camera. What could she possibly say that would erase or absolve the whole I-slept-with-another-man-while-I-swore-my-love-and-devotion-to-you bullshit? Thoughts of the two of them naked, their limbs entwined, was too much to bear, so Ivan took a larger than normal gulp of the bubbling wine, hoping it would erase the mental image his last thought had created.

With perfect timing, Ivan's phone buzzed against his hip indicating a late night text, something he'd become all too accustomed to. He grabbed the phone from his waistband and chuckled at the irony as he read the message:

Fontainebleau room 1020 if you're up for it.

Ivan didn't want what was being offered. He wanted what didn't exist anymore. *Go!* his mind screamed at him. A heavy sigh escaped his mouth, and his head dropped back against the chair. He didn't want to go to the Fontainebleau, nor did he want to be alone. But the pull of a physical connection and the moment's peace it offered was too good to refuse. Ivan could hear his inner freak's laughter and feel his anticipation building as his fingers flew across the phone:

I'll be there in 30.

As he hit send, an overwhelming sense of disgust leached through his body. This was not him. This wasn't what he wanted, or who he wanted to be, but it was what he needed. The feel and touch of a woman was the only thing that could bring him close to what he'd once had with her—the nirvana he craved to experience again, if just for an hour. Sex was the drug for the heartache that plagued him. It let him feel like he wasn't fucking them, he was fucking her, and it was a sweet escape until it was over and he was once again consumed by the guilt and shame of his desperation. The rougher the sex, the more intense and real the mirage of her.

Ivan hated his addiction. He hated that he was strung out on it all the time. But at least he was doing *something*. This was a step farther down the road, which was progress. And life was about progress, right? Nearly paralyzed by guilt, his body tried to stand and ready itself for a night of carnal lust, but his heart pleaded with him not to. Love had kicked the shit out of him…twice. But as far as he was concerned, this overwhelming feeling of loss and foreboding was something he'd have to fuck his way through until the pain eased. *Go ahead and fuck her,* the freak encouraged. Ivan silently conceded, and the freaky little bastard exulted, suddenly free to get his next fix from one of the many nameless, meaningless sexual drug dealers that prowled Miami Beach.

Ivan tossed back the last of his wine and hurried to get dressed before he changed his mind. It enraged the freak when his conscience interceded, and in return the cruel monster would make him suffer. Rifling through his closet, he grabbed a pair of dark jeans and a black T-shirt he'd gotten from his sister one Christmas. *Trust me. I'm a doctor*, it read. The irony of the message wasn't lost on him. It took less than a minute to brush his teeth, pull his hair into a loose ponytail and daub his neck, chest, and crotch with cologne.

Still battling with the freak, but knowing he was fighting a losing battle—these days the freak *always* won—Ivan grabbed a wad of twenties from the nightstand drawer and gave himself the onceover in the full-length mirror. He snatched his aviators from the hall table and hung them from the neck of his T-shirt. It was the same routine over and over again. He knew the freak wouldn't be sated again until the light of day. He started down the hall to the elevator, but something nagged at him.

"Condoms! Shit." He hung his head and scolded himself as he darted back to his apartment. The weight of the tiny box felt like a hundred pounds in the palm of his hand, but it was a hundred pounds he had to bear. He needed his fix, and he hated himself for it.

CHAPTER 4

"Down With the Sickness"

"Fuck me like you mean it!" the woman screamed as she lay on her back with her knees pinned to the bed on either side of her head. Ivan was more than happy to oblige.

The sounds of flesh slapping against flesh confirmed that he was fucking her just as she'd asked. Hard thrusts took him deeper and deeper into her, numbing his mind and satisfying his body. His triceps ached from supporting his weight as he thrust in and out of her, and his calves began to scream for mercy as they flexed harder and harder to keep pace.

"Do you like it when I fuck you hard?" he yelled back, not caring what answer she'd give. He didn't need to hear it because it was written on her face. This girl was no different from any of the others he'd bedded. They all liked it hard, fast, and dirty.

"Tell me what you want," she moaned, looking up at him from between her parted legs, her eyes begging him to give her more.

Her words were the same he'd heard dozens of times, and like all those other times, he did as he was told. Pulling out of her, Ivan sat back on his heels. "Turn around and get on your knees," he demanded.

Without hesitation, she flipped over and got on all fours, presenting herself to him in the dim morning light. There was no heartfelt plea from within his soul asking him to stop now, only a deep-seated carnal lust. His fingers dug into her hips as he pulled her to the corner of the bed and stood behind her. A primal hunger took control of his body, possessing him fully. With punishing force, he pushed himself into her from behind and unleashed a flurry of intense strokes, each one driving her wilder than the last. Faster and harder Ivan pummeled into her, inching himself toward that piece of heaven that justified his actions. Euphoria swept through his limbs and a sense of self-worth crept back into his life with every inward stroke. As the feeling took effect like a drug, Ivan's body began to quiver with anticipation.

In one fluid, automatic motion, he reached for the strands of bleached blond hair that taunted him as they danced back and forth across her naked back. He fisted her hair in his hand and wrenched her neck to the side, taking solace in the throaty moans and gasps of pleasure that escaped her cherry red lips. Their bodies trembled as they neared the ecstasy they craved: the ten seconds of complete and utter inner peace that only an orgasm could provide.

"Where do you want it?"

"On my face. Oh, God…" She groaned and looked over her shoulder at him as she licked her lips.

Dirty. I like it. Before she could finish whatever thought had entered her filthy little mind, Ivan tugged her hair and brought her to her feet in front of him only to force her to her knees a second later. Reacting to his unspoken demand, she tore off the condom and began to stroke him hard and fast. Her mouth formed an O as she readied herself to catch her prize.

Looking down at her and seeing the sultry glint in her eye was enough to push him to the edge. He coiled with approaching sexual delight, and his body prepared to reward him the only way it could. Taking control, Ivan reached down and pushed her away, stroking himself furiously as current after current shot through his body. He gripped his cock tighter and with one final stroke he exploded, covering her body and face with the rewards of his release. Still on her knees in front of him, she took him back into her mouth and began to milk him dry, but the sexual morphine had already started to wear off. With his eyes squeezed shut, Ivan tried to savor the feeling for as long as possible, but it soon faded, along with the vibrant colors and euphoric sensations that had come with it.

"I should put you on speed dial," she said as she ran her fingers around her mouth. It seemed less an attempt to clean up and more an attempt to savor.

But her voice sounded like nails being drawn across a chalkboard, and it was the final nail in his coffin. As the last remnants of his fix vanished, Ivan snapped back into his dull tragedy of a life, one painted in muted colors and flooded with dark feelings.

The petite blonde with a top-notch plastic surgeon at her disposal got up from the floor, threw a towel in his direction, and wandered off toward the bathroom. "I need to wash up."

Ivan stood motionless — still in the same position where he'd experienced a bit of respite — and shut his eyes, hoping to wake up from this nightmare. Minutes passed, and he opened his eyes slightly… nothing. His surroundings remained the same. He opened his eyes a bit wider…still nothing. That's exactly what this was. Nothing. It was the black void of nothing that his life had become.

He didn't notice that the blonde had returned to the room until she cleared her throat to get his attention. He turned his attention to her and was surprised to see she was dressed and stepping into her shoes. "You can stay if you want to, but I have to go."

Yanked from his fog, Ivan reached for the towel she'd tossed his way and roughly cleaned himself as he gathered up his clothes. "No, I should be going too."

"Do you need cab money?" she asked as she stared into the mirror and reapplied a thick layer of rich-girl-red lipstick.

He snorted a soft laugh as he pulled up his jeans and buttoned the fly. "No, I'm good. Thanks, though."

She turned back to him, her small purse tucked under her arm and a parking valet claim ticket and some cash in her free hand. "All righty then…"

Ivan didn't reply but kept on with the task of getting dressed. He turned his black T-shirt over in his hands and looked up at her.

"You wouldn't mind giving me a ten-minute head start, would you? I'd hate for anyone to see me at this hour with a shadow," she said. "You know how fast gossip travels in Miami Beach."

He put his arms through the T-shirt and pulled it over his head. "No problem."

"I knew you'd understand." She blew him an air kiss and turned her sky high heels toward the door. Just before the door clicked shut he heard her call out to him, "You're a doll!"

He blew out an exasperated sigh and dropped his chin to his chest. He knew every second spent in a hotel room doing the freak's bidding, getting his goddamn fix, was accruing a debt that was tallied by the minute, one his soul might never repay.

He slipped on his flip flops, picked up his sunglasses, and tucked his keys and wallet into his pockets. He took a quick glance around the room and then went to the bathroom, where he splashed cold water on his face and ran his hands through his hair. In the mirror was a virtual stranger with beads of water dripping down his face and over his beard. He hated the man who stared back at him. *God, who have I become?* His guilt worsened. He splashed cold water on his face over and over.

Washing away your sins, are you? the freak taunted.

Ivan picked up a towel and scrubbed it hard over his face, then released a heart-wrenching, guttural groan of a yell into the cotton he held tightly over his mouth. The day-to-day stuff was hard, but this shit—the aftermath of one of these sex sessions—was when the real torture began.

He tossed the towel to the floor, raked his hands through his hair, and wondered if it had been ten minutes. *Screw that.* He put on his sunglasses and stalked out of room 1020 toward the elevator bay. The doors slid open, and Ivan stepped into the elevator. With a whoosh he sped toward the ground. Then, as he had so many times before, he traversed the hotel lobby, sidestepping the throngs of people as they made their way toward the counter. An overwhelming sense that he was on trial for the act he'd just committed burdened his heart, and for a moment it froze him in his tracks. He was suddenly unsure he had the strength to face the day.

Fuck it. Progression! The freak roared in victory, but Ivan couldn't shake the feeling of foreboding that had settled in his soul. He looked out through the glass front doors in the lobby, cracked his neck, and ran a hand though his just-fucked hair, wishing he'd taken the time to find his hair tie. But there was no avoiding it. His life wasn't going anywhere.

Muggy air embraced him as he stepped through the doors, raised his arm, and hailed a taxi.

"Where to?" the cab driver asked.

"South. Just head south."

CHAPTER 5

"Miami"

"Please make sure your seat belts are fastened and your tray tables are in their upright and locked position. We are beginning our final decent into Miami. Flight attendants, please take your seats. Thank you."

The sound of the captain's voice jolted Jaden awake. *God, I love redeye flights.* She stretched out every inch of her body, thankful that the seat beside her was unoccupied, and relished the momentary rush of endorphins that accompanied the lengthening of her muscles. Once her mind shook the cobwebs clean, excitement coursed through her. It had been too long since she'd seen her best friend. Tasha's last visit to L.A. had been more than a month ago. Jaden told herself that her jittery stomach was all about the anticipation of catching up with a dear friend. But she knew that wasn't true. Though it still scared her to death, the chance of running into Ivan now tantalized her.

She'd done her best to distance herself from all thoughts of him after her attempts at contact had gone unanswered, but this time it felt different. Calls and texts and emails could be ignored, but if she happened to run into him, that would be her chance. Surely she could convince him to hear the truth of her terrible mistake. It was still terrible, of course, but not the betrayal she'd once thought it was. She'd just been confused and lonely and way, way too drunk. Growing agitated, she ran her hands through her hair. She needed to explain things face to face. If Ivan saw the truth in her eyes and heard it in her voice then maybe, just maybe, he'd forgive her. For everything.

The plane came to a stop at the gate and Jaden gathered her things with renewed purpose. This was going to be a good trip. She'd be a new woman by the time she returned to L.A. She smiled to herself, fighting off nerves, as she walked through the nearly deserted airport to baggage claim, where she retrieved the two oversized suitcases she'd packed for her extended stay.

After wrestling her bags off the conveyor, Jaden found a pleasant looking Latin man with a thick mustache who held up a sign displaying her name.

"Hello," Jaden said as she waved to the man.

"Good morning, Ms. Thorne. May I take your bags?"

Feeling a bit of guilt, she looked over her shoulder at the two large suitcases behind her. "Thank you. That would be great."

"You're welcome," he replied.

As she watched him manhandle the bags, she was struck by a vision of Ivan, who had toted her bags everywhere they went, no matter how heavy they were or how feminine they looked. Her breath caught in her throat as the doors slid open to reveal the warm Miami morning. Jaden breathed in deeply, then exhaled, feeling overjoyed with the familiarity of being home. She pulled her oversized sunglasses from her purse and slid into the backseat of the waiting black sedan.

The car sped off to the hotel that would act as her temporary abode for a few days until her two-month lease started. She'd entertained the idea of staying with Tasha and Micky, as Tasha had insisted, but in the end she'd decided that might be a bit too much togetherness. Hearing Tasha *talk* about their fantastic sex life was plenty without having to experience it for weeks on end. She'd convinced Tasha this was the way to go after she found the perfect little condo for rent, which Tasha was bound to enjoy as well. She smiled again at the thought of her friend. All she wanted to do was let her hair down and lounge by the pool while sipping mojitos with Tasha. To just be. *A girl can spoil herself now and then, can't she?*

The towering concrete buildings whizzed by and yielded to the glistening blue of Biscayne Bay. As they crossed I-195, Jaden felt surprisingly at ease. Everything felt so familiar, so right. She'd loved her time in Miami and suddenly realized she hadn't just been missing

Ivan or missing Tasha, she'd missed being here. The car exited the causeway and returned to land, and in no time it had pulled up at the hotel.

Jaden adjusted her sunglasses and was surprised at the flow of people and cars coming and going from the hotel. It was still pretty early.

"Here we are, ma'am. The Fontainebleau," the driver called.

Yet another surge of emotion pulsed through her body, but this time she knew it was nerves. Feeling uncertain, she realized she had no idea what she'd do if she saw Ivan, and she felt exposed, leaving the safety of the car. Would she have the presence of mind to initiate a conversation? Would he?

The driver made quick work of unloading her bags and handing them off to the bellman. He waited while Jaden fished a tip out of her wallet, then with a nod, he and the car disappeared. She followed the bellman inside and took her place in line for the desk behind two eager tourists who were anxious to get on with their sightseeing. She scanned the bustling lobby, finding the entrance to the night club where she and Ivan had spent many nights with Tasha and Micky. She closed her eyes and smiled at the flood of memories. The sights, the sounds, and the essence of Ivan's signature scent filled her with nostalgia, which grew stronger and stronger until it seemed as if he were standing right next to her.

Feeling a jolt of panic, Jaden opened her eyes and caught a passing glimpse of a man moving through the lobby. The shape of his body seemed familiar. Long, tousled brown hair swung across the back of his black T-shirt in time with a distinctive and recognizable gait.

No. She was letting her mind run away with her. Why the hell would he be at a hotel, let alone this early? Yet she couldn't break her stare as he walked farther and farther away, the alluring scent fading with every step he put between them. Just as he reached the exit, he stopped as if he'd hit an invisible force field. *Turn around, dammit!* She willed him to shift just an inch. She needed to confirm it wasn't who she thought it was.

Slowly, the man turned, ran a hand through his hair, and scanned the lobby as if he were looking for someone. As his profile came into view, Jaden's eyes locked on his arm and the bulging vein that ran down his bicep. *Oh, God!* He lifted his face toward her, revealing a trimmed beard and a pair of aviator sunglasses. *Oh, God, no!* Her stomach plummeted as her eyes came to rest on the one thing she could never mistake for anyone else's: his face. His hair was a bit longer, and she'd never seen him with more than a few days of scruff before, but there was no mistaking it. Behind the beard, it was Ivan.

Shit... With what she hoped was a nonchalant move, Jaden ducked her head as her heart jumped into her throat. *Please, don't let him see me,* she pleaded with the universe. And after a few moments, when she dared raise her head enough to steal a glance in his direction, her prayers had been answered.

CHAPTER 6

"Creep"

$\mathcal{I}$van smiled as he stared down at a pair of freshly plumped lips. He'd even impressed himself. This was a job well done.

The sixty-year-old beauty smiled up at him. "Thank you, doctor. You're just as good as they say you are. I must admit, you're the best I've ever had."

"Is that right?" He looked down at her with a cocked eyebrow and a smirk.

"Oh, God, yes. You're definitely the best. I didn't feel a thing."

"In any other situation I would take offense to that, young lady."

"Oh, behave!" She laughed and continued to marvel in the mirror at her new lips. "I'm old enough to be your mother."

"Behaving is no fun, Mrs. Merandez." He offered her his hand and helped her up from the chair. "Let Liz know when you want to come back in."

"I will. Thank you."

Ivan left the procedure room and went back to his office where he found his assistant, Liz, waiting for him with a curiously sexy look on her face. As he passed her on the way to his desk, he couldn't help but steal a look at her ass.

"Mrs. Merandez is ready to go," he informed her as he took a seat behind his desk. "Give her seven months before you schedule her for a refill. What do I have next?"

"Next you have a medical club membership consult in room two with a VIP from Panama and his wife."

"Okay, I'll get right to it." When Liz didn't reply after a moment, Ivan knew there must be something more she wanted or needed. He was notorious for an occasional missed signature here or there, but normally she'd just leave the chart on his desk with a Post-it note attached. "Is everything okay? Did I forget something?"

"No, you're up to date," she said with a laugh.

"Good to know. Gold star for me!" And yet she still stood there, now giggling like a schoolgirl. Ivan looked at her closely, trying to judge her disposition.

Finally she got around to her point. "So, umm…The word on the street is you're back with your ex."

Ivan froze, his heart sending a rush of sweat down his back. Relying on his go-to defense mechanism, he laughed. "What? Where did you hear that?"

"Well, a friend of mine is friends with someone whose sister is the concierge at the Fontainebleau."

"Huh. Is that right?" He wiped a quick hand across his now-sweaty brow. "The Fontainebleau, you said?"

"Yep. She also said she overheard Jaden talking on her cell. She told someone she was staying there a few days until her apartment was ready."

His mind went into overdrive as it tried to absorb this information. Jaden was back in town, *at the Fontainebleau*, and apparently staying for a while. "Well, I can assure you I don't know anything about that. That book is closed, my dear."

"Good!" Liz replied a little too quickly. Catching herself, she shuffled from foot to foot. "I mean, it would be a shame if you were off the market."

Her flirting caught him off guard — or maybe it was the bombshell she'd just dropped on him. If there was one thing he knew for certain, office romances were a big no-no. He thought he'd always been clear on that point, but then who knew what he'd been doing with himself lately. Slipping behind his best poker face he replied, "I'm still out there and still shopping." Good God, he needed to clear his mind. He could barely keep himself in his seat.

"Good to know." She smiled a smile that had no place in an office as she turned to leave. "I'll go get the next patient ready for you."

What the fuck? The door shut with a resounding thud. Was Jaden moving back to Miami? What about the show? Liz's words were no doubt the sounding bell for another fresh round of heartbreak. He'd fooled himself into thinking Jaden's life was in California now and that Miami Beach — much like their dead relationship — was a thing of the past for her. Sure, she'd visit Tasha and Micky every now and then, but dodging her on the occasional weekend was a breeze. However, having to avoid her at every turn would be a much bigger challenge.

"Shit." Ivan scrubbed his hands over his face and pushed back his hair. Would Jaden come knocking on his door? The distance between California and Florida had made it easy to ignore her attempts to reach him, but on an island that was only 18.7 miles wide, if she wanted to see him, she would be unavoidable. He sighed again. Would that be so bad? He'd been so desperate to stop the bleeding that he'd never really tended to the wound. He'd avoided communication with her at all costs, but maybe if he just dealt with it and talked to her, he'd be able to move on.

Then again, maybe Liz's intel was all wrong. Maybe he was freaking out over nothing. *Liz!* the freak demanded.

"No!" Ivan shouted into his empty office. He was hanging on by a thread, and this was no time to give in to his addiction. He needed to simplify his life, not let the freak complicate it any further. Better to just medicate the fucker now before he did something stupid like picking up the phone and calling her. Reaching for his cell, he dialed the concierge at the front desk of the hotel that housed his office.

"Hello?" The man's smooth voice came over the phone.

"Hey, boss. It's Ivan. Tonight I'm going to need a bottle and a table."

"Any particular table, sir?"

"Doesn't matter. I'll be there at ten." With that, Ivan hung up the phone and slumped back in his chair, his mind numb.

The door opened and Liz peeked in. "Doctor, they're ready for you."

Yesssss! For a moment he forgot she was a lawsuit waiting to happen and narrowed his gaze. "Thanks," he purred.

"Anything for you."

The sultry sound of her voice, so ridiculously inappropriate for a work environment, snapped him back to reality. He sighed as the door closed behind her. His job was to help people feel better about themselves. Too bad he couldn't make it work for himself.

Ivan went to the sink and washed his hands. As he did so he looked himself over in the mirror and shook his head. He looked as shitty and shell-shocked as he felt, but his schedule had no space for any kind of meltdown today, big or small. Good thing he was a pro when it came to quarantining unwanted thoughts and emotions these days, because tucking away the idea that Jaden was in Miami Beach behind door number three was now a priority. He smoothed his hair back, fastened it into a ponytail, and then went in for his next consult.

For the rest of the day, he moved from appointment to appointment, allowing himself no time to think about anything but IV administration, hangover cures, libido-boosting cocktails, and the new club membership he'd secured with the Panamanian VIP couple. And when that was done, the hours between his last patient and his ten o'clock reservation downstairs were occupied with reading patient labs and catching up on dictation.

At nine thirty he gave himself permission to clock out. In an instant, as he shed his lab coat and powered down his computer, the freak began to whisper his intentions for the night that lay ahead. Ivan had spent all day keeping himself together, and he was exhausted. He was left with nothing to fight off the freak, if he even wanted to. Now it was time for surrender to the sweet sedation only the freak knew how to deliver.

CHAPTER 7

"Dream, a Little Dream"

Jaden looked down at Ivan and ran her hands through his hair. His tongue lavished her pussy as waves of pleasure crashed over her. He had one hand wrapped around her legs, holding the flimsy bikini bottoms aside, while the other fondled her naked breast, teasing and twisting her nipple between his thumb and forefinger until she thought she'd burst.

"Oh, God, Ivan! Don't stop!"

Faster, he worked his tongue in and out of her. She writhed with the sensation as warm ocean water pooled around them. Her body tensed and trembled as she inched closer and closer to orgasm. She grabbed a fistful of hair and forced his face hard into her. The sensation of his rough beard against her soft flesh was unfamiliar, but not unwelcomed, and she ground harder into him, forcing more of his tongue inside. Each stroke brought her closer and closer, and just when she thought she could take no more, he spoke to her, replacing his tongue with his fingers without breaking rhythm.

"Come for me, baby," he commanded in a low, sexy tone as he continued to stroke her from the inside out. "Now."

At the sound of his voice she began to tremble. When he curled his fingers inside her and flicked his tongue over her clit, she shattered. She couldn't even pull in a full breath and instead managed only short, desperate gasps as he continued to tease her with his mouth and fingers. She rode out the first orgasm, tugging at his hair as her legs trembled around his head.

"Do it for me again, Jaden. I want to hear you scream," he demanded as he worked her toward a second, more powerful climax.

"Yes! *Yes!* Oh, Iv—"

Beep. Beep. Beep.

She sat up in bed, disoriented by the sound and the aftereffects of the amazing feeling that had eluded her for so long. After a moment she realized where she was (in her new condo) and that she was alone (no Ivan). She glared at the bedside table and slapped the alarm on her phone silent. She blew out a heavy breath and fell back into the comfort of her new bed. She hadn't known dreams like that were possible.

Dreamgasm? She nearly managed a giggle. People have wet dreams all the time, she reminded herself. She'd just never experienced one quite so intense or with such a spectacular finish. Dreaming of Ivan in such a raw, sexual form had awakened feelings she'd tried to pack away months ago. *There's something to be said about the beard and longer hair. He looked bigger, too—his arms were huge. God, I wonder what else has changed?* Fighting off a wave of sadness, she shook her head, hopped out of bed, and headed for the shower.

As the water ran over her body, she thought about what she wanted versus what she needed. She *needed* to tell Ivan the whole story, to explain how she'd lost her way, been foolish and selfish, but her heart had held fast to him. It had kept her true. She *needed* to tell him how sorry she was and beg for his forgiveness. He needed to know she hadn't slept with Damian and that no amount of emails, text messages, or phone calls could convey how sorry she was. And what she *wanted* was for everything to go back to the way it was, for them to make their peace with what happened. She *wanted* Ivan to forgive her and pick up where they'd left off, rebuilding on the foundation she hoped still existed. *But wants and needs are not the same*, she reminded herself. *And it's the needs you should attend to first.* If she could just get Ivan to listen, if she could know for sure that he knew the truth, maybe then she could find her way to peace no matter what the outcome.

Jaden stepped out and wrapped herself in a towel. Should she tell Ivan she was in town, or should she rely on fate to place him in her path? What if he'd already heard she was there? Four days wasn't long, but word traveled fast in South Beach. She and Tasha had enjoyed a pool day already, so of course Micky knew she was in town. Jaden wasn't sure how she felt about the fact that Ivan and Micky had become such great friends, but she supposed it was comforting to know Ivan had at least one good friend left who didn't want anything from him—didn't have any underlying business plans or shady, self-promoting motivations. Further proving his loyalty, Micky had made it clear he had no interest in being in the middle of this situation and planned not to discuss either of them with the other. But still…There was probably some kind of bro-code necessity that would eventually wear him down.

She needed coffee. Fortunately, in addition to furniture, her condo had come equipped with a convenient little single-serving coffee machine, with all the flavors of the coffee rainbow to choose from. She tucked the tail of the towel deeper and tighter under her arm and headed for the kitchen. Just a few quick clicks and a couple of minutes later, she moved into the living room with a steaming mug of coffee in hand. She stood quietly, enjoying the view from the condo. Finding this short-term sublease had been a stroke of luck. She smiled down at joggers on the boardwalk below. Not long ago, she'd run along that same path and wondered what the view looked like from this building. Now she knew.

Jaden pushed open the sliding glass door, stepped out on the tiny, standing-room-only balcony and looked out across the bay. For six months she'd been away from Ivan, and from Miami Beach. She'd played out countless scenarios and had a thousand imaginary conversations with him, trying to sort out how she might actually begin reconciliation. None of her phone calls, texts, or emails had done anything other than prove her tenacity, but even if he hadn't read them, she hoped he realized she wasn't ready to let him go.

And though she continued to have moments of self-doubt, when she wondered whether she'd ever deserved Ivan at all, something about seeing him her first morning back in town at the Fontainebleau had galvanized her resolve. And in a way, her dream this morning now pushed her forward as well. She had to speak with him. She had to try in person to get him back.

What if he's dating? What if he's dating a lot? *What if he really doesn't want you anymore?* Jaden thought for a moment and realized she could live with the answers to those questions, no matter what they were. Of course he was dating. She'd be surprised if he wasn't. And perhaps he'd even met someone else to care for. She'd be crushed, but she had to know. At least then she would know for certain whether she'd have to continue to live alone with the consequences of her actions. Perhaps she'd finally mourn the loss of true love and move on. That's what she *needed*.

What she couldn't live with would be more of his evading and her being forced to pretend that everything was okay, in both her personal and professional lives. She knew he had never let Irena back in, even if only to cinch up a relationship gone bad with an ounce of closure, and eventually Irena gave up. And because she did, Ivan had been available when Jaden came along. *Huh*…It wouldn't be easy, but what they had was real and worth saving. She had to try. No giving up.

A warm breeze kicked up around her, as if the universe approved of her tactics. She couldn't control Ivan's actions, but she was definitely in charge of her own. No matter how long it took or how desperate it became, the way forward for her, the way to find herself again, would be to seek Ivan's forgiveness until he told her there was no chance in hell he could ever love her again.

She wasn't giving up. Jaden took her coffee back inside and picked up her phone.

I miss you.

CHAPTER 8

"Love and Memories"

"Asian chicken salad and a pitcher of water, please," Ivan said. He handed the menu back to the waiter without having looked at it. He'd been here a hundred times, and a hundred times he'd ordered the same thing.

"Yes, sir."

This was his go-to place for good food and people watching, and Ivan found himself once again nursing a sexual hangover from the night before. He could still remember how the incessant drone of the synthetic music had reverberated off the club's walls as Ivan and the freak sat patiently.

Quietly cling¬ing to the control and good judgment that had become rare at this stage of the game, Ivan's eyes never stopped moving as he observed and assessed potential partners for the debauchery the freak demanded.

Redheads, brunettes, blondes, Cubans, Asians, and a particularly spectacular African American woman — all the colors of the flesh rainbow had swarmed the dance floor, writhing in perfect harmony. Many of them met his eyes as he watched. No doubt they scoured the perimeter for the next unsuspecting, unlucky bastard — the next future ex-husband, Sugar Daddy, or Mr. Right Now. As long as he had cash money to spend, he was their next victim. This immediately ruled them out, as this was not what he had in mind. Ivan, and whether he liked it or not, the freak, was looking for sex, not a social climber. They worked in tandem, eliminating women one by one. Only a no-strings-attached, no-games-to-play sexual drug dealer could give him what he needed to bandage the hole ripped back open by the recent return of heartbreak personified.

Blonde on the left. Ivan eyed the Eastern European girl in the light blue dress shaking her shit and making aggressive eye contact.

Come on, Ivan pleaded with the freak. Ten minutes into it she'll be asking about financials and what she gets for fucking us. Even though you can bounce a quarter off her ass, she ain't worth it.

Okay, black girl on the right in low cut jeans and the white shirt.

Ivan's eyes raked over the dark beauty on the dance floor. When the music transitioned from low beats to high energy, her body flowed along fluidly, indicating some real talent. He nodded appreciatively as the delicate flower budded into an erotic fruit that tempted him without mercy.

No, no, no... the freak interrupted. *The redhead with the boy shorts and her tits out.*

Ivan found the rocket cutting the rug five yards away. When she felt his eyes on her, she began running her hands up and down her body. *She would be insane. I want that. We need that.*

Uff... He hated when the freak made him an active participant in chasing his addiction. There was always less guilt, less responsibility when they pursued him. This game, this pretending he had a choice, that the freak wouldn't ultimately decide his fate for the night, was miserable. But the news of Miami Beach's latest arrival made him desperate, which was worse than being miserable. How many would it take to satiate this unquenchable thirst and numb his heart?

As the DJ continued through an endless playlist of shitty techno music, Ivan had sat back and contemplated the gauntlet the freak laid before him:

Blonde with the IQ of a golden retriever but the ass of a thoroughbred.

Black girl with an ass shake that would move mountains.

Or the redhead whose lustful stare could melt the foundation that held marriages together.

Left, right, up, down, over, under — it didn't matter. No matter how he tried, the thought of Jaden in town made him yearn for the ultimate release and some kind of magic amnesia for what could and should have been. The possibility of her being close enough to touch made him hope to cross her path, but the idea of actually seeing her scared the living shit out of him. Did she deserve a response to all her attempted contacts or did she deserve him fucking all three of these girls tonight and reaching the highest sexual oblivion possible to drown out the idea of her?

He'd surveyed the room one last time and then surrendered, allowing the freak to unleash himself and clip all three ladies who had tempted him. With a flick of his hand, an unmistakable stare, and a tip of his head, he'd beckoned them one by one to his table. He'd done his alter ego's bidding and then retreated into himself, letting the freak take control.

Later that evening, the three gorgeous women, their flesh slick with sex and sweat, had all tangled together in a night of debauchery. It had taken a swarm of nameless women to satisfy the freak this time, and he was beginning to feel a little out of control. Nameless, faceless women were all he had left, and evidently they were beginning to lose their effect. Every encounter was more aggressive and deviant than the last, and with each one, he lost a little more of himself. He was becoming tolerant to the drug he'd used to numb the pain, just as the source of his pain had drawn near. What would he do when the high wore off completely and he was left with a gaping wound in his chest? That scared the shit out of him, too.

Desperate now to change the direction of his thoughts, Ivan diverted his attention away from last night's debauchery and back to the present. He'd indulge in some good old therapeutic Lincoln Road people watching, a pastime that had always seemed to soothe what ailed him. He watched as what appeared to be a fifty-year-old rollerblader rolled by wearing a gold thong that matched his skin tone. *Interesting.* Seconds later, a Rastafarian guy with dreads hanging down to his ass meandered by asking for spare change. *Boring.* But what did catch his attention was the dark-haired girl looking sexy as hell in a red dress and oversized sunglasses. *Now we're talking.*

But on second look, his heart began to pound in his ears like a drum. This wasn't some beach bunny out for a stroll. It was *her*, the one who'd kicked him in the proverbial nuts six months ago before a crowd of all their friends. The one who, minutes later, had torn his still-beating heart from his chest in the parking lot. The one who'd stripped him of his very essence. And the one who still controlled everything he was and all he wanted to be.

As she closed the gap between them, he began to tremble in anticipation, nervousness, or fear—he couldn't discern which one. But it didn't matter, because he had to get a grip on whatever inconvenient emotion was bubbling up to the surface. He looked down, covering his face with one hand and fumbling with his phone in the other. He tried desperately to blend in. He wasn't ready for any form of contact, and he didn't know if he ever would be.

After a moment he couldn't help but raise his head and admire her—the way the red dress clung to her curves—as she passed. But his admiration was cut short when the freak offered his two cents: *Lying, cheating bitch.*

Maybe talking to her was what he needed to let go and move on. He had to quit punishing himself before he spiraled further out of control. *I know what you need…*

"Here you go, sir."

"Thank you," Ivan managed as he looked down at his favorite dish. But the sight of her had caused him to lose his appetite. The freak roared in his ear, urging him to go and lose himself in his next fix, but he ignored the beast's taunting and allowed his mind to fill with thoughts of what could have been.

If she hadn't shattered their happily ever after, they would've been planning a wedding together this very moment. They'd be the "it" couple of South Beach, enjoying fantastic careers and the fruits of all their hard work. His new practice would be the freedom and joy he'd wanted it to be, not just the endless grind of additional work it sometimes seemed like. She would visit him in Miami Beach to soak up the sun and relax, and he would go to L.A. to spoil her and provide temporary relief from the hustle and bustle of entertainment life. Their lives would have been full of colors and feelings that blinded with their brilliance, not this mundane, sepia-toned half life he was living.

Nevertheless, he was thankful for everything the business had required of him lately. He ran both hands through his hair. Where he was and what he was doing was his dream. Yes, Jaden had for a time been part of that dream, but he still had a plan, a purpose. Before things fell apart with her, he'd believed he was putting everything he had into his career, but without her, he'd discovered how much more he could make himself give. The current ahead-of-schedule success of his new practice was no doubt a direct result of the pain and heartbreak he'd experienced. He was a master at masking his devastation with determination, and he'd funneled all his extra time and creative energy into his work. He shuddered to think what he and the freak might become without it. It was a bittersweet return for such an investment, but if she hadn't crucified him and their relationship, he wouldn't be where he was now. And it was exactly where he wanted to be, wasn't it?

He knew in his heart it wasn't. It had sounded like a lie from the moment he formed the thought, but her gigantic clusterfuck of a mistake had kept his storybook ending from being written. There was nothing he could do. Suddenly Ivan knew there was no way he could survive with her in his Miami Beach bubble. He had to know why she was here.

Wait, mistake? Is that what it was? But he shook the thought from his mind as he hailed a passing waitress. *It was so much more than a mere mistake.* He handed the waitress a fifty-dollar bill and pointed to the Rastafarian still scrounging for change outside. "Could you box this up and give it to that man right there, please? And you can keep the change."

And with that he strolled off in the direction opposite the one she had just come from, hands in his pocket and a hole in his bleeding heart.

CHAPTER 9

"Somebody That I Used to Know"

"Let's go, bitch!" Tasha yelled as Jaden scurried up the concrete steps that led into Bianca.

"I'm coming, I'm coming, but these shoes are killing me," Jaden replied, pointing to her new pair of four-inch black patent heels.

Tasha smiled and offered her an arm as they entered Jaden's former workplace through the large, wooden doors. Jaden grinned and closed her eyes for a moment as she soaked in the familiarity. "Ooh, they have new drapes," she commented. "The classic white is a nice touch."

Tasha rolled her eyes, but was prevented from delivering her next snarky comment by Geoff's voice.

"Jaden Thorne!" He burst through the kitchen's double doors with a dramatic flair and darted across the dining room to greet her.

"Geoff!" she cried, wrapping her arms around him. "I've missed you!" And in that moment, she realized she really had.

"How have you been? What are you in town for—business or pleasure? And where's—" Geoff caught himself and smiled apologetically.

"I missed my friends and my favorite kitchen," Jaden explained. "The show is on hiatus."

"Well, I'm glad you're back. It's so good to see you! And it's nice to see you as well, Tasha. She's one of our regulars, you know," Geoff added with a wink. "Are you going to be here long?"

"I'll be here two whole months," Jaden announced, looking around. "I'll be relaxing, but you know a chef can't stay out of the kitchen for long…"

"Don't tease me!" Geoff warned. "We'd love to have you back any time you want!"

"You just let me know, and I'll be sure to be available."

"You're the best!" Geoff wrapped Jaden in another hug, then returned to his business self. "Let's get you ladies some food."

He led them to a table and motioned to a waitress standing by the bar.

"I want you to try everything," he instructed as he pulled out their chairs. When they were seated, he nodded politely and took his leave.

"Susan!" Jaden yelled as she looked up at the waitress. In an instant she'd jumped up from the table. "I thought you'd moved! And you changed your hair! I love it."

The now-blond server hugged Jaden and blanketed her with a torrent of words. "It's so good to see you. I was working downtown, but it didn't work out, and Geoff was nice enough to give me my old job back. Ohmygod, I watched every one of your shows! Is Damian as hot in person as he is on TV?"

The happy reunion turned cold as Jaden felt a rush of bad vibes sweep through her at the mention of Damian's name. "Ahh…" she managed as she struggled to recover.

"I hear he has his own show now," Susan continued. "God, I can't wait to see it." She looked up for Jaden's response and seemed to misinterpret the look on her face as insult. "But I bet it's nowhere near as good as your show!"

"Ha! Well, we'll find out, won't we?" Jaden said with a weak smile, turning one of her earrings between her fingers.

"So what's good? What do you recommend?" Tasha interjected.

Jaden took the opportunity to sit.

"Everything!" Susan blurted as she began to prattle on about the new menu. "Your tuna is the only thing Geoff kept from the old menu…"

Jaden turned to listen to Susan, but she didn't hear her. Her mind had wandered back to the day she'd returned home from dotting Damian's eye with her fist. A plain brown package had nestled amongst her accumulated mail, and its Miami Beach return address had piqued her interest, though she should have known better. Nevertheless, she'd torn open the package and emptied its contents onto her kitchen counter. And at that point her heart sank even lower. She'd found a red box with a red bow and a card addressed to Baby Girl. Unease had bubbled in her stomach, and she'd debated just throwing everything away. Clearly the gift wasn't meant for her now.

But she'd known in an instant she couldn't do it. She could never discard something Ivan had sent her. She'd reached for the box and pried it open. Opal earrings, and around each opal were four flippers and a tiny head. Tears had come to her eyes and, torturing herself, she'd picked up the white envelope and opened it with an unsteady finger. When the trembling subsided, she removed the card and began to read:

> Jaden,
>
> My life is forever changed by the grace you've instilled in it. Just as I feel you've completed me, I want to complete a collection I started some time ago. I hope you enjoy these sea turtle earrings! Love is beautiful and so are you. A life without you is a life without purpose. You're the happy ending in my book of purpose, fantasy, and hope.
>
> ~Ivan

She'd wiped her eyes with the back of her hand and sunk to the floor. It had been hours before she could move.

"So what will it be, Jaden?"

Susan's words cut through her daydream and brought her back to Miami Beach, but she realized part of her was still crushed on her L.A. kitchen floor. She'd had no idea what to do with those earrings, and since then she'd had little idea what to do with herself.

"Ahhh…Surprise me!" she declared, as cheerfully as she could, ignoring the pang of guilt in her stomach.

Susan looked as if she might say something, but just nodded and turned from the table. Jaden watched as she wound a sure path through the dining room. Once she'd disappeared through the swinging door, Jaden let the tired smile slip from her face and took a ragged breath.

"What was it this time?" Tasha asked.

"Hmm?" Jaden looked back at her friend.

"You're pitiful," Tasha said with a sigh as she handed Jaden her linen napkin. "And your mascara is beginning to run."

Jaden took the napkin and dabbed at her eyes.

"What triggered the tears this time?"

Jaden shrugged, sniffed, and adjusted her posture.

"Is it just being here at Bianca? Geoff? The mention of your famous tuna? Is there some big, secret memory lingering under one of these tables that I don't know about?"

"Very funny," Jaden said with a sad smile.

"I told you we should go somewhere else—"

"It's fine. I wanted to come here."

"So what was it?"

Jaden reached touched her earring. "Nothing."

"Nothing. Really?" Tasha crossed her arms and leaned in.

"Okay, it's everything," Jaden confessed. "My relationship with Ivan started in this very spot, in the kitchen of Bianca. And I'll be damned if I let it slip away without a fight!" She looked down as a new wave of tears threatened. "God, Tasha, you'd think I'd have cried all the tears of a lifetime in the past six months, but nope. Just when I think I've got a grip and can venture out in public, they spring up to remind me how fucked up all this is. When is it going to get better?"

"You want the sympathetic best friend answer or straight-up truth?"

"Can't I have both?"

"They're pretty much the same. The only real difference is in the delivery."

"Straight up."

Tasha cocked her head. "Reaaally?"

Jaden took a sip of her water and gave Tasha the all clear.

"It'll get better when you get off the pity party speed train you've been riding for six months and fucking forgive yourself," she said. "You call him every week, text him how many times a day? How many emails, Jaden? And what do they all say? *I'm sorry! I'm an awful person! Please talk to me! Please give me another chance!* You're stuck between begging him and punishing yourself, and that's enough. You screwed up, *big time.* You lied, you kept secrets, and now six months later you're still surprised he's not ready to deal with the needy girl who just wants him to call her back?"

"I—Jesus, Tasha."

"I'm fucking serious, Jaden. If you can't forgive yourself then how in the hell can you expect him to forgive you?"

Jaden focused on straightening the silverware at her place.

"That's where you start, at least," Tasha continued, her voice softer now. She reached for Jaden's hand. "Forgive yourself and get your shit together. Because, honey, you may look great on the outside—maybe a little too thin and you could use a good conditioner on that hair—but you're a lost little girl on the inside waiting for a man to make you whole again. I need you to *please* remember who the hell you are! You are Jaden fucking Thorne, and this mopey, weepy bullshit is played out."

Jaden ventured a look at her friend.

"*I* wouldn't forgive you if every time you called me you were a puddle of sorrow and wah-fucking-wah!" Tasha added dramatically, releasing Jaden's hand.

She managed a laugh and began to shake her head.

"I'm serious. You're fucking annoying, and this is me being supportive." Tasha finished with a flourish.

"Wow. How did I get so lucky?" Jaden deadpanned.

"It's called tough love, sister." Tasha winked. "Get your groove back, your mojo, your moxie—whatever you want to call it. Let's not forget Ivan's part in this, eh? He wasn't exactly Captain Communication there for a while, and—not that it excuses your behavior—but this didn't happen in a vacuum. Climb down off the cross and find some way to forgive yourself, and then maybe you'll be able to do what you need to do next."

"What's that?"

"I'm not some common fortune teller, Jaden. I don't have a clue what's next. But I imagine it's the equivalent to putting away the comfy clothes, ice cream, and sappy play lists and pulling out the Manolo's—"

Jaden cleared her throat and kicked Tasha under the table *with* her Manolo.

"*Ow!* I'm talking metaphorically, girl."

Jaden laughed and rolled her eyes.

"All I'm saying is that you can't keep doing what you're doing and expect a different response. This approach hasn't worked, so you fix you, and then maybe you'll have the opportunity to fix this mess with him."

"I love you, Tasha."

"I know you do."

"Why didn't you let me have that months ago?" Jaden asked as she took a deep, cleansing breath and put her napkin in her lap.

"Because you wouldn't have heard me, and I'd have had to admit you to some rehab place for exhaustion and dehydration or whatever tired celebrities check into rehab for these days. I didn't want to push you over the edge."

Jaden sighed again, and the two erupted with laughter just as Susan delivered their first course.

CHAPTER 10

"When Worlds Collide"

"I'll take a large iced coffee—black with no sugar, please—and a packet of almonds." Ivan gave his order to the petite, freckle-faced redhead behind the counter. It was his standard request to satisfy his daily Starbucks obsession, but the cute barista's smile didn't hurt either. Her sparkling eyes probably gave him more of a jolt than the coffee would anyway. He'd consumed thousands of gallons of the stuff during medical school, and his body had become mostly immune to its effects.

As a growing group of groggy patrons lined up for their caffeine hit, he moved aside to wait for his order, shuffled the songs on his iPhone, and readjusted the collar of his too-tight dress shirt as he looked around. Beads of sweat had already begun to form on his forehead, and he cursed himself for not wearing something cooler. At the height of the tourist season, the place was crawling with several typical Miami Beach species. A group of *Overcompensatauruses* sat at a table just outside the glass window, dressed in cut-up bright tank tops drenched with fresh sweat. This particular species was known for trying to attract any passersby to their weekend-warrior bodies. A couple *Ineedfreewifiotops* sat in the corner and lounged on the sofa as their hands moved over their laptops. Also scattered here and there throughout the coffee house were the *Iamtooimportantapuses*, who radiated their self-worth for all to see.

But what finally caught his attention were a stunning pair of legs belonging to a rare and beautiful creature: the *Comeandlickmypus*. This species appeared to be prissy, uptight debutantes, but it's a little-known fact that in certain circles they were among the most adventurous nymphomaniacs the world has ever known. This was the type of gorgeous, uptight bitch that most other girls wanted to knock the hell out of. They were the ultimate creature with Grade-A reputations, able to consume a man in one swallow. No male would ever be the same after bedding a *Comeandlickmypus*. Ivan knew this firsthand. It was this exact species that most effectively fed his addiction.

The *Comeandlickmypus* looked up from her magazine and caught him staring at her from across the room. But neither broke eye contact. *Interesting.*

After a moment Ivan dragged his eyes away. Attempting to silence the freak's voice, he adjusted his ear buds and turned his attention back to his oversized cup of caffeine, which was now being mixed with ice. He prayed the growing bulge in his pants wasn't noticeable.

"Here you go, sir," the cute barista said as she handed him his order. "Have a great day!"

"Thanks." He nodded and turned toward the condiment station. As he did so, he caught a glimpse of the beautiful creature with her eyes still locked on him. Her intense gaze burned his skin and coaxed the freak closer to the surface. *Yes!* It roared in delight.

Ivan did his best to ignore the voice *and* the temptation staring at him from across the room. He busied himself with prepping his coffee: four Splendas and a splash of skim milk. But just as he started toward the door, his phone pinged an alert, interrupting his music and his exit. He stopped at a nearby table and sat down to scroll through the text messages and emails that had accumulated since he'd left home. Business, work, business, work…it never stopped.

Bringing the iced coffee to his lips for another sip, he found the same pair of aqua blue eyes boring into him. The *Comeandlickmypus* wore heavy, black-framed glasses, but they only served as an enhancement to her stunning eyes. Smiling, he nodded to the brown-haired woman who he guessed to be in her mid to late thirties, though she didn't look a day over twenty-five. Her gray business suit and white blouse screamed power and professionalism, but it also hinted at secret sexual desire.

Do it! Louder and louder the freak cried to be set free, and Ivan became weaker and weaker with each passing glimpse and casual smile. He sipped his coffee and focused on his phone, trying to fight back his urges and silence the freak's voice. But when the last of his beverage was gone, he was left with a decision to make. He could murmur a string of curse words as he made his way to the exit, or he could man up.

Fuck it! Let's play this one out, he decided as he stood up from the table. A sly smirk played at the corner of his lips and his eyes danced across the crowd, over to the bathrooms, and back to the leggy *Comeandlickmypus* who he found watching his every movement. She nodded slightly, acknowledging his gesture.

Game over. Ivan took the ear buds out of his ears and wound the cord around his phone before slipping it into his pocket. Then he headed to the bathroom at the back of the coffee house. The freak roared its approval with every step he took — this would be his most daring conquest yet, and Ivan could feel his control slipping away as the alter ego took over. He took a path that led him past her table, and felt her hot stare. A curl at the corner of his mouth confirmed what her eyes were saying. They were both in for one hell of a ride.

He entered the bathroom and closed the door behind him, but left it unlocked. In two long strides, he crossed the tiled floor, stood in front of the mirror, and splayed his hands across the cold granite counter. But when he looked in the mirror, the reflection staring back at him was unfamiliar. It was the face of the freak. Anticipation coursed through his body, and he wondered if she would join him or reject him. He wanted her to follow him in. It didn't matter that he didn't know who she was — or that she might know who *he* was. He'd grown more and more reckless since the day his addiction took hold.

You'll thank me later. The freak rejoiced when the door clicked open and the sound of high heels clacking against the floor reverberated through the space, seeming impossibly loud. As he heard the lock slide into place, Ivan broke the stare he'd held with the desperate man in the mirror and allowed himself a glance at the woman behind him. His heart beat rapidly as his body readied for the feast of which he was about to partake.

Wordlessly, she approached him, sliding her hands under the back of his suit jacket. With her jet black stilettos, there was no need to stand on her tiptoes for her mouth to reach his ear. The tip of her tongue snaked out from between glossy lips and traced the curve of his ear, sending ripples of anticipation through his already aroused body. As her hands came to rest on his chest, he turned toward her and tilted his head, exposing his neck. He shuddered as her hands ran down his stomach and came to rest on the bulge that strained against his pants. She stroked him over the fabric and let out a warm gasp against the nape of his neck. He loved that she took control.

Her hands moved to his waist and she hooked fingers through the belt loops on his pants. With slow and deliberate movements, she slid down the length of his body. Then she was on her knees in front of him. Her eyes—half lidded and full of need now—looked up at him through the naughty-librarian glasses perched on the bridge of her nose, and she smiled as she managed his zipper. When the warmth of her lips surrounded his cock, Ivan thrust forward, driving himself into the back of her throat. Undaunted, she took him even deeper into her mouth. She released him just enough to tongue the sensitive spot beneath the head of his cock before taking in every inch of him again and again and again, each time deeper than the last. Harder and faster she worked him, and she didn't object when he grabbed her hair and forced his cock deeper inside her mouth.

Fuck yes! Before he lost all focus, Ivan glanced back at the mirror and watched as the unfamiliar reflection mouth-fucked this beautiful brown-haired woman without regard. Then the ringing of his phone diverted his attention away from the show. The sound of Frank Sinatra and the screen, which read AVOID, told a tale of heartbreak starring him as the main character. He hadn't been able to delete *her* phone number, but he had changed the name associated with it to remind him that he needed to avoid *her* at all costs. The ringtone, however, remained the same. He couldn't even bring himself to change that.

Avoid! his mind yelled, yet his heart fluttered as the ringtone continued to play. Meanwhile the freak, oblivious to the phone, begged for more. *More!*

Ivan's hands dropped to his sides and his head fell back against the wall, his eyes cinched shut. When Frank finally stopped singing and the call went to voicemail, Ivan opened his eyes and stared at the beige ceiling above him. *What have I become?* This wasn't how he treated people, and it wasn't how he treated himself. This unexpected interruption—the one-two punch of Frank and AVOID, along with an enormous wave of remorse—suppressed the beast that had possessed him for so long, and for an all too brief moment, Ivan felt like his old self. When he turned back to the mirror and noted a hint of familiarity in the face of the person staring back at him, he knew he'd hit rock bottom.

He looked down at the woman, still on her knees in front of him, and suddenly the sight repulsed him. He couldn't take it any more. He couldn't move quickly enough as he pulled his dick from her mouth. She looked up, her face full of confusion.

Ivan scrambled for an excuse to forfeit the situation gracefully, as if that were even possible, and stuttered his lame explanation. "I shouldn't have...I don't usually..."

"Shame," she said as she stood and nonchalantly stepped up to the mirror. "Wife?" she asked as she reapplied her lip gloss and smoothed her hair.

"No." He pulled his pants up, still as hard as a rock, and zipped.

"Maybe next time, hmmm?"

With a quick backward glance over his shoulder, Ivan uttered the only thing that came to mind. "Never say never."

He pulled the door closed behind him, leaving her in the bathroom—probably not for long, but he wasn't about to stick around to find out. Ivan thought he noticed more than a few grins and chuckles from patrons sitting near the bathroom in his rush to leave. He pushed through the doors and into the brilliant Miami morning, relishing the warmth of the sun as it beat against his face. He took a deep inhale and felt like he could breathe again. He looked around for a moment. Something was different. As he looked off toward the horizon it hit him: For the first time in a long time, his gray world appeared a bit pastel. A hint of color played just outside his field of vision. He had some thinking to do.

CHAPTER II

"Someone Like You"

The message-waiting icon taunted Ivan over and over again. This wasn't just *any* unread message. It was *her*—a person he hadn't spoken to in more than six months. Granted, he'd left many of these messages unheard and unanswered since the night she shattered his world, but for some reason this message, without even being heard, had incited a riot of emotions inside him.

The freak was still pissed that he'd cut short his encounter with the *Comeandlickmypus*, but Ivan now channeled all his need and tension back into the one thing that had always served him and his body best: exercise. He ran harder and faster along the path than usual, working his muscles and flooding his system with endorphins. He ran as if he were trying to outrun something, and maybe he was, but he was thankful that after a while his head and his thoughts began to feel less deadened and fuzzy.

As he ran flat-out along the path, he noticed the sky darkening with a distant thunderstorm, and after a moment he realized he'd noticed the contrast between the brilliance overhead and the looming darkness for the first time in a long time. *She'd* stripped him of more than just his heart and soul. Colors, smells, sounds—his awareness and appreciation of life and the things around him had all been lost six months ago. She'd left him without his usual zest, truly destroyed. He smiled as he gripped his phone in his fist, pumping his arms as he ran, the thin cord of the ear buds bouncing against his chest and classic rock blasting in his ears. For some reason, he felt better.

However, neither the run, the sky, or the darkening clouds overhead could distract him from the voicemail. It promised him the possibility of his life back, Ivan realized. But whether he'd be putting something to rest or breathing it back into existence, he wasn't yet certain he wanted to know. Redoubling his efforts to force all thought from his mind, he turned up the volume and pushed himself harder. But not even AC/DC could tear him away from his spinning brain.

A storm was coming.

He thought back to the day of the meltdown at The Bath Club, and he could feel the despair, loneliness, and anger build with every passing moment. The thought of her in bed with Damian, the douchebag's hands touching places he'd once held sacred, made Ivan sick to his stomach. But after a time, memories of the nights he'd spent in Jaden's embrace and the mornings filled with laughter tempered his hatred. What was he missing? How had this happened? He missed her and found himself wishing for a way to forgive her.

But there wasn't a way. The betrayal was too big. It changed everything, and that's what left him with no idea what to do. Why did he even want her anymore? It was as if some parts of him just refused to face the truth. He watched as little by little the looming storm clouds stamped out all hints of vibrancy from the sky. He'd tried to compensate for her loss by making his business his life. What had kept him busy with a constant to-do list in the planning phases now consumed as much of his time as he'd give it with the new practice up and running. There was always another opportunity to pursue, another patient to follow up on, someone's business to court.

The transition from aspiring, business-minded doctor to CEO of his own company had left him basking in the good life — money coming in, setting his own rules, plenty of prestige. Or at least he'd dreamed it would be the good life. He'd achieved what he'd always wanted, but much to his disappointment, he now knew no career accomplishment could fill the emptiness of his personal life. A whole new level of fancy cars, big apartments, expensive dinners, and lavish trips did nothing to cure his inner sickness. And yet he couldn't stop. He had no idea what else to do, so he just worked harder.

Ivan shut his eyes and indulged in the breeze that accompanied the brewing storm. *Goddamnit!* He exhaled and opened his eyes. The phone weighed heavy in his hand, and he turned it over and checked again that the message was still there. It was. Through gritted teeth, he pushed his body even harder. How had he reached this point? How had he wandered so far from the person he thought he was?

"Mind if I join you?" The sultry Spanish accent of the freak's first conquest still echoed in his ears. Visions of the Latina bombshell danced across his mind, causing his cock to twitch in his shorts. The white cocktail dress she'd worn had rested mid-thigh and her ample cleavage had been bursting out the top of the sweetheart neckline. Chestnut hair with streaks of blond cascaded down a beautifully tanned back and sat in waves on the shoulders of her athletic build.

"Yes, please do," he'd purred and pulled out the chair next to him. He'd accepted her company as she slipped in beside him at the bar during one of the many Miami Beach charity events that filled his schedule. He was someone in demand, after all. Yet after three months without *her* and no relief in sight, he'd been wallowing in self pity, and his body had begun to demand that he find another way to compensate for his emotions. He needed to feel something...anything. What he wouldn't give to experience the vivid colors, beautiful smells, and brilliant feelings of love that had once filled his heart.

After two drinks, their small talk had turned suggestive. He'd marveled at her beauty, and she'd spoken words of passion that made him hard. An inner urge began to build, which at first seemed alien in nature. It had been the first time since *her* that his urges threatened to consume him.

Back and forth they went, dancing to the tune of lust, desire for the inevitable mounting with each graceful step across the dance floor.

"Why don't we get out of here? We can go back to my place and crack open a bottle of wine," she'd suggested, and in the same moment she'd turned on her heel, leaving him to catch up to her.

That had been the exact moment his addiction started. With that simple little sentence she'd provided him an alternative to the black-and-white life he was living. Nothing material had satiated his need for happiness, or even normalcy, and no amount of work could keep his demons permanently away, but the promise of flesh had awoken the freak and his carnal needs. But how could he have known where this would lead, what he would become? It was just a casual drink at a beautiful woman's house.

Before he knew it, they were in a cab and her version of a nightcap would soon become his heroin, the only way to numb, at least for a time, the growing pain that resided deep within his chest. They'd spilled out of the backseat of the taxi in front of a lavish beach house. Step by step he'd followed behind her and paused at the front door, wondering what could come from this act of desperation. What he'd found on the other side of her door was his medicine. His drug. A soothing numbness, and yet also the only way to find any energy or color or beauty in the world. This gorgeous Latina had tempted his body and also gifted him his first fix.

Through all the faceless and nameless sex he'd had since she'd initiated him, he'd never been able to bring anyone back to his own bed or even kiss her on the lips. These two intimate gestures he kept in reserve for someone more deserving, but the freak hardly seemed to notice. It made him feel he'd preserved a part of himself, although lately his grip on that seemed tenuous as well. He knew if he fell much further, the facelessness and namelessness of his fixes would be his undoing.

His legs burned and his lungs felt like they were going to explode when he finally eased up on his pace and began to downshift. A few minutes later, with his hands on his hips, he tried hard to catch his breath and walked in a wide circle as he shook out his limbs.

"Fuck it," he whispered to himself. His mind, his body, and his soul: all three were suddenly ready to hear what Jaden had to say. As inexplicably as he'd started down the road to his addiction, he now prepared to turn around and start back. He turned the phone over in his hand and paused the music. He stared for a moment at the red message-waiting icon that had tortured him all day. When he touched it, a voice he hadn't heard in an eternity began to ring in his ear.

"Hey, Ivan. It's Jaden. I'm in Miami Beach for the next two months, and I'd love to see you. Any chance you could make some time for me?" A pause left him trembling on shaky, tired legs, but then she continued. *"Please call me back and let me know."*

Her voice swam through him, igniting emotions he'd believed long dead. He tried to discern one feeling from the next, but couldn't. Rage was trumped by happiness, which gave way to disappointment and then a flicker of hope, but in the end, anger trumped all. He was lost. Should he be happy? Should he be angry? Should he call her back? His mind did gymnastics as he tried to decide what to do.

Could he stomach speaking to her, let alone seeing her? She'd left him a broken man, alone to pick up the pieces of his shattered life.

He longed to call her back. Maybe forgiveness would make things right in his world and he'd be able to move on. But something in the back of his mind, some unfathomable force, told him *no*. Lightning crackled across the darkening sky. *You need to move forward. Never break your promise to yourself. You have a plan.*

He'd been through this painful routine once before with Irena, and he'd somehow managed to get through it. It had taken time to heal the wounds, time for him to forgive, but now he harbored no ill feelings toward her and was at peace with everything that had happened. *Time* was the key word there. Perhaps he needed to give this more time. Jaden had stung him much deeper than Irena ever had, and he knew if he gave in to what he wanted, his ability to get what he needed might suffer. He loved what they'd once shared, and he didn't want to taint it by playing the blame game...But who was he kidding? *She* was the one at fault, the one who'd been unfaithful to him. Jaden had made a conscious decision to be with another man while they were together, and then she'd lied about it.

Ivan stopped his circling and yanked the T-shirt out of the waistband of his shorts. He used it to wipe the sweat from his face and his neck, and then with an aching heart, he started a text message to avoid:

> Jaden, Your star no longer shines in my sky.
> Love for you still flows through my veins,
> but it no longer reaches my heart. I wish you the world. ~ Ivan

He read and reread the message a dozen times, contemplating whether he was being stupid, childish, smart, or all of the above. All three made perfectly confusing sense to him. After a while he felt confident that he would never know whether texting her was the right answer, so he just pushed the send button.

Thunder rolled across the sky, and the first drops of rain began to fall. He took a deep breath and turned toward home, scrolling through his music until he found the perfect tune. As he began to run, Adele began to sing.

CHAPTER 12

"Against the Wind"

"Is everything okay, man?"

"This side of the dirt," Ivan mumbled, studying his menu. Oliver's was their usual hangout, and this lunch was long overdue. After avoiding Micky for weeks, he'd texted him yesterday after his mind-clearing run.

"Don't bullshit me." Micky looked across the table, concern on his face.

Ivan glanced up from his menu. "What?"

"I know you know that Jaden is back in town."

"So?"

"So...I just assumed when you texted me and set up this little meeting you were...you know..."

Ivan put down his menu and leaned back in his chair. "Here we go again."

"I thought maybe you were ready to talk. Look, I'm just trying to help you. You haven't been the same since you and Jaden split up."

"Would you be?"

"Of course not, but it's been six months." Micky threw his hands up in exasperation. "What's your deal? Business is good, and the women are plentiful. That's not a bad life, if you ask me."

Ivan studied him for a moment. If it had been anyone else, he would've gotten up and left. He couldn't even have a simple lunch without being reminded of *her?* But this was Micky, the only person he could confide in—not that he had. How many times had they seen each other since the proposal debacle? He couldn't even count, but he'd never so much as acknowledged what had happened, no matter how many times Micky tried to bring it up.

Yet now his words struck a nerve. "Yeah, I know," he grudgingly responded. "What's your point?"

"Have you even talked to her since The Bath Club?"

"No, I haven't. But she texts or emails me almost every day. Yesterday she called and left a voicemail."

"Every day?"

"Yep."

"And you've never talked to her or responded to her?"

"Nope. I don't need to."

Micky laughed and shook his head. "I think maybe you do."

"She made her bed. She can lie in it."

"Do you really think that? How do you know if you haven't even talked to her? Maybe there's something you don't know."

Tasha and Micky had clearly overanalyzed this whole Jaden situation. Hell, Tasha was probably the one to put him up to this line of questioning. And they were questions better left unanswered. Once, just once, he wanted a day of peace—one day of not thinking about her. Was that too much to ask?

As if fate knew he needed a temporary reprieve, the waiter appeared. But even after he'd taken their orders and collected their menus, Micky still wore the same questioning look. Ivan's reprieve was short lived.

"What else is there to know, Micky?" Ivan's voice lowered into a defensive growl. "What would you do if Tasha slept with someone else—some rich kid, pretty boy who had more money than brains? After all the time and energy and love you poured into your relationship—not to mention keeping the rest of your life on track and starting a new business—she slips into bed with her co-worker the second you turn your back, the same co-worker she pissed and moaned about incessantly."

Micky sat back with his arms crossed over his chest while he vented.

"Now, top that off with the fact that you knew you wanted nothing more than to be with her for the rest of your life, and to prove it you got down on one knee in front of all your friends and offered her a commitment that in her eyes was nothing but a joke." Ivan rubbed his hand over his face and readjusted his chair before continuing. "Actually, wait — let's take a step back because that's not even the worst of it. For the real kicker, she doesn't tell you what she's done and instead takes you to her parents' house, people you instantly fall in love with. Then she proceeds to fuck you after she's been with another man and carries on as if she hasn't a care in the world. This is a girl you would have done anything in the world for…" He paused for a moment to stare at the table.

"I probably could've forgiven her if she'd just been honest with me up front," he finally added. "That's all I ever asked of her. But no, she couldn't even do that. She jerked me along for God knows how long, screwing me and fucking him." Removing his sunglasses, Ivan set them on the table and stared into Micky's eyes. "Let me ask you this. Would you give a damn about her after everything she did, and would you listen to some bullshit story about how she was sorry?" Ivan silently dared Micky to respond, but he said nothing. "I didn't think so!"

The men stared at each other across the table, and Ivan reveled for a moment in the fact that he felt better, lighter after vocalizing six months of pent-up frustration and anger.

"But you know what?" He dropped his head in defeat. "My problem is that I do give a damn, and I hate myself for it. I still love her more than I should, and I'd probably still do anything for her if I let her get close. But I don't think I'm strong enough to suffer another blow from that woman. That's the reason I can't talk to her — not because of anger or spite, but for fear she would crush me…again." Ivan sank back in the chair and put his glasses back on.

"You feel better, man?" Micky asked after a moment.

Ivan started to chuckle. "Yeah, man. Well played. I didn't think you were that clever."

"What the fuck does that mean?" Micky asked with narrowed eyes. But he was smiling.

"Nothing," Ivan said with a laugh. "Thanks, man, I needed that. It felt good."

Micky sat back in his chair, smiling. "We aren't all Superman, my friend."

"No, we're not."

"But that doesn't mean we don't all have kryptonite to deal with."

Ivan blew out a heavy sigh.

"You did a good job practicing on me, but I suggest you talk to the person you really need to talk to," Micky encouraged. "I think maybe it's time you give her a call back."

Ivan reached for his glass of water and took a long sip. "Maybe I should, man. Maybe I should."

CHAPTER 13

"Keep On Loving You"

"Leave it alone! Every damn time I try to do your hair you end up ruining it." Tasha smacked Jaden's hand away from the curls at the back of her head. "I'd think you'd be used to this by now. Don't you have people doing your hair all the time?"

"Sorry. I'll stop," Jaden huffed. "I guess I'm not as afraid of you as I am of Kat."

"Ha. Don't push your luck," Tasha countered. "I could be scary if I needed to be."

Tasha set back to work, feverishly pinning curls in place, and Jaden tried to get her mind on the night ahead. She'd been back in Miami for nearly two weeks, but she hadn't been particularly successful at turning her mind off to recharge just yet, so it was just as well that Kevin was already scheduling her for events. Tonight's gala, hosted by Jaden, would feature a who's who of fabulous Miami restaurants, each showcasing their signature dishes.

"Are you excited or are you nervous?" Tasha asked. "Why aren't you saying anything? I can't wait to see you in action, but I'd be a nervous wreck if I had to speak in front of all those people. They have you plastered all over the invite, and I bet the after-party will be awesome too."

"It'll be fun, I hope. Maybe it'll be the distraction I need. I should focus on my professional life for a change."

"That's a fantastic idea, and in light of that, I have one rule for tonight: *Ivan* is not to be thought about, spoken about, or even mentioned." Tasha slurred his name distastefully. "I don't want you moping over that text he sent you like you did all day yesterday. Remember what we talked about at Bianca? You fix *you*. Get your groove back. This is a big night for you—a big deal. You need to be in top form. Besides, it's his loss for blowing you off. He doesn't even have the decency to call you back? A fucking text message? Asshole."

Jaden rolled her eyes and snickered.

"I saw that." Tasha tugged at her friend's hair. "Not one word about him, got it?"

"Ouch!" Jaden laughed, feigning pain. "Okay, I get the point. No more Ivan talk tonight."

"Besides—" Tasha lowered her voice to an almost-whisper "—from what Micky told me last night—Aw, shit!"

Jaden felt a stab of anxiety. "What did he tell you?"

"Damn it, Micky is gonna kill me. You know he doesn't want to be in the middle of this."

"I'm going to kill you if you don't finish what you started," Jaden threatened. She turned in her seat to look at Tasha. "Tell me."

"Please don't say anything. Micky would kill me if he found out I told you, and I'm sure Ivan would have a few unsavory words for him." She took a deep breath and exhaled loudly. "Micky had lunch with him the other day, and Ivan finally talked about you. He vented about everything. Micky didn't tell me all the details, but the gist of it is that Ivan still loves you and wants to talk to you. But don't you dare say anything!"

Perplexed and a little angry that Tasha hadn't told her sooner, Jaden felt a warm rush of emotion spring up in her chest and flood her cheeks. "What did he say exactly? I can't believe you didn't tell me!"

"I don't know, really. And anyway I wasn't supposed to tell you. Micky didn't tell me a whole lot. He just kind of skimmed over the conversation." Tasha gave her a half-hearted smile. "I think he knew I might slip up. That man knows me better than I know myself."

"That's all the detail you got out of an entire lunch conversation? That he may or may not call me?"

"Well, Micky said Ivan let it all out, and he thinks that he's going to cave and call you."

"I'm calling Micky right now."

Tasha grabbed Jaden's hand as she reached for the phone. "Oh, no you don't. I'll never hear the end of it if he finds out I told you. And anyway, it doesn't matter. You've done all you can. You're focusing on yourself now, remember? Just relax and give it a day or two. I'm sure Ivan will call when he's ready."

Jaden drew in a breath and prepared to protest, but what was the point? Instead she turned in her seat so Tasha could finish her hair, but her mind had trouble returning to tonight's event. "What the hell am I going to do now?"

"Stop being such a drama queen," Tasha teased, twisting another curl. "Forget that this conversation took place and carry on with your evening."

"Yeah, right."

"Second, you're going to slip your pretty little ass into that outrageously expensive dress the studio sent over, and you're going to enjoy the evening."

"Well, I don't —"

"And then," Tasha said, cutting her off, "we're going to celebrate at the after-party for a job well done. We haven't been out on the town in ages, and I know you're going to love this new club."

"God, I hope so. Maybe Ivan will —"

"Hey!" Tasha screeched. "No mention of him, remember?"

"Fine," Jaden conceded. Just knowing Ivan was at least thinking about calling lifted a huge weight from her shoulders. Perhaps she could enjoy the evening, or at least lose herself in her work. It had been far too long since she'd had any fun. "They gave me a VIP table and unlimited complimentary champagne. I'm sure we can do some damage with that."

"That's what I'm talkin' about!" Tasha said with a laugh. "Okay, all done. I just have to finish my makeup, and I'll be ready to go. You'd better get dressed."

Jaden stood up and eyed the teal dress that hung from the back of the bedroom door.

"That's what they want you to wear?" Tasha asked, eyes wide for the eyelash curler.

"Yep. Doesn't seem like enough fabric to me. I might as well get a pair of fishnet stockings and hooker heels to go with it."

"Sex sells, girl. Work it," Tasha said with a smirk. "You'll make it classy, I'm sure. And it's Miami. They just didn't want you to get too hot! Who knows, you might even get lucky tonight."

Jaden laughed and rolled her eyes. "Yeah, that's what I need. A seedy hook-up."

"I think getting laid might be the best thing for you."

Jaden pulled the dress off the hanger and unzipped it. "I can see the appeal, but come on, really? I'm not going on the prowl at this network party."

"Why not?"

Jaden stepped into her dress and gave Tasha a look. "Well, letting my personal and professional lives collide has not been the best move for me in the past. And I'm going to let the veil of mourning the love of my life slip here, in Miami Beach of all places? Why should I risk certain gossip, which would spread like wildfire, mind you, for a one-night stand?"

Tasha turned in her chair. "Do you remember what happened the last time you hooked up with a guy?"

"Of course I do." Jaden looked away and wrestled into her dress.

"And what was that?"

She stopped her shimmying and gave Tasha a death glare. "What the hell, Tash? Are you serious?"

"I didn't mean — Shit." Tasha rolled her eyes and shook her head. "Not that time. The time before."

"I met I—"

"Ah! Don't say his name, remember?" She pointed a makeup brush at Jaden. "You got a whole lot more than lucky that night. Let's focus on that, shall we? Who's to say it can't happen again?"

Jaden let out a sigh and tugged at the tight dress. She turned her back to Tasha and pointed to her back for a zipper assist. "I love your optimism, Tash, but I don't think it's a good idea."

"I think it's the best idea."

She gasped as Tasha yanked up the zipper. "I'm sure you do."

"Just promise me if you meet someone you like that it's not out of the question."

She's got a point.

No fucking way.

"Stop it!" Jaden shouted, effectively shutting down both the meddlesome voices she'd worked so hard to exorcise from her head and Tasha at the same time. "I'm not promising anything. I have three goals tonight: get through this evening with my pride intact, maybe earn a little more industry credibility by being a goddamn professional, and come home with a teeny bit of self-respect. If I do that I'll be way ahead of where I ended up after my last work-related event. Getting laid is not on my list of shit to do right now."

Tasha smiled and turned back to the mirror. "That's a to-do list I can get behind."

Jaden moved to stand next to Tasha as she checked out her hair and makeup one last time. "Good. Thanks for the help with my hair. Kat would approve! And remind me of my to-do list later, okay?"

"In case you meet some hot guy?"

"No, you little shit." Jaden laughed and yanked on a tendril of Tasha's hair. "In case I forget and turn into a drunk, weepy mess, wracked with guilt and insecurity after too much tequila."

CHAPTER 14

"Sympathy for the Devil"

"I can't tell which one of you is more excited," Micky said as he drove the two giggling ladies north on Collins Avenue. "You'd think you'd never been to one of these things before."

"This is so exciting! For you...I'm so excited for you, I mean," Tasha gushed.

Jaden smiled. "I'm glad you're coming with me. It's been a while since I had a good date to one of these!"

Micky looked at Jaden through the rearview mirror. "So, are you ready to make your official debut as Ms. Miami Beach? You're running the show tonight, right?"

"I'm still not sure about this whole Ms. Miami Beach thing, but it seems I am sort of in charge tonight. I'll be doing a lot of talking anyway." She laughed and hoped she didn't seem nervous, which she was. "A night on the town is exactly what I need right now," she added.

The Jeep rolled up to the curb in front of the hotel. Burly security guards, menacing PR reps, and a plethora of photographers flanked both sides of the red carpet, waiting for the next big-money image to stroll by. A little closer to the doors, women in gowns and men in tuxedos smiled prettily for the cameras.

"Ooh, I might be underdressed," Micky quipped as he gestured to his shorts and wrinkled T-shirt. He leaned over and kissed Tasha. "Tear it up, girl!"

A stab of pain shot through Jaden's heart as her friend blushed and smiled. She wasn't jealous of what her friends had, of course, but she did regret what she'd so stupidly lost. Once upon a time Ivan used to kiss her like that, and she could still scarcely believe she'd never feel his lips on hers again. But she remembered her promise to Tasha and swept those thoughts from her mind.

"Call me if you guys need a ride home!" Micky said.

"Will do," Tasha called over her shoulder as they slid out of the car.

"I love you, baby."

"Love you too." Tasha leaned back in to give Micky another kiss goodbye.

After he pulled away to weave through the crowded parking lot and back to the street, they took a moment to smooth their dresses and admire one another. "You look *hot*, Tasha!" Jaden announced as she produced a laminated guest pass from her clutch and handed it over.

"Umm…thanks," Tasha said, eyeing the crowd up ahead. "Obviously you do too. And not just because I did your hair."

"C'mon. You'll be just fine," Jaden told her as they headed toward the doors. Flashes exploded against the night sky as they approached, and photographers vied to get a clear shot. Jaden maneuvered Tasha past two massive security guards and around an overeager photographer, then stepped onto the plush red carpet. She gave her friend's hand a squeeze, took a deep breath, braced herself for her first real Miami appearance as the headliner, not a plus one. From her humble beginnings as a chef just in from Colorado to the host of her own TV show, she'd come a long way. The thought was both daunting and invigorating.

"Jaden! Ms. Thorne!" a voice called from the crowd.

Jaden turned to find a frazzled woman pushing toward them, wearing a plain gray dress and an earpiece. She offered her hand. "I'm Judy, and I've been assigned to work with you tonight."

"It's nice to meet you, Judy," Jaden replied, shaking the woman's hand. "This is my friend Tasha."

"It's a pleasure." Judy nodded. "Okay, so I need you to do a quick photo op, then we'll get you inside."

"Okay."

Judy ushered the two women to the gigantic banner full of sponsor and charity logos alongside the all too familiar network logo. Tasha stood off to the side as Jaden took her place in front of the banner. From the corner of her eye, she watched as Tasha lost herself in the bright lights and commotion. Jaden remembered how overwhelmed she'd been at her first network event. *Nothing a drink or two won't fix!* She smiled to herself as the cameras began to click.

When the flashes had faded, Jaden stepped down from the platform and rejoined her friend. "Just smile and look sexy."

"You mean there's more?" Tasha asked, eyes wide.

"The worst is over." Jaden linked arms with Tasha and together they walked toward the ballroom. "Let's get a drink."

Judy, who had somehow snuck past them, appeared at the entrance to the ballroom. She held up a hand to stop them even as she spoke into her headset. "She's already done…He's here? Now?"

Jaden listened intently. Something about the tone of the woman's voice caused goose bumps to rise on her forearms.

"Mr. Gibbs requested it? Are you sure? Okay…" She listened for another minute before turning her attention back to Jaden. "Ms. Thorne, I hate to ask, but we need you to take a few more pictures. Mr. Gibbs has arranged for a special guest to be here, and he's just arrived. He would like you to take a photo with him."

"Not a problem," Jaden replied, relaxing her shoulders. Ahh, it was definitely a work night. But she'd survived the first photo op, so a few more pictures weren't a big deal, were they?

"Can you come with me, please?"

"Of course." She turned to face Tasha. "Go ahead without me, and I'll be right back."

"I'll get us a drink." Tasha nodded bravely.

"You read my mind," Jaden replied as a cold hand encircled her wrist and swept her back outside.

"All right, they're here. Let's get you back out there for your shot." Judy somehow magically parted the crowd and urged her to the platform.

Blinded by hundreds of flashes, Jaden caught barely a glimpse of the person who stood smiling for them. Something about his profile seemed familiar, and then it hit her like a ton of bricks. She struggled to make her face neutral as he turned and looked at her—not just in her direction, but directly at her. *What the fuck is going on here?*

Judy tugged at Jaden's hand. "Come along, darling. Time is wasting. We've got to get you inside as soon as we can."

A wicked glint lit up Damian's eyes as Jaden joined him on the step and repeat. "Let's hear it for tonight's host and my former partner in crime—one of Miami's top ten hottest celebrities, the lovely and beautiful Ms. Jaden Thorne!"

That son of a bitch! Jaden was no stranger to being put on the spot, but this was too much. Kevin hadn't felt this was a relevant detail to share with her? What the hell was Damian even doing in Miami? *Asshole.*

"What the fuck are you doing here?" she growled through gritted teeth.

"Such foul language from a talented mouth. I'm sure you can find better things to do with it than curse at me," Damian whispered.

Jaden shuddered. "You have no right to be here."

"I heard you were single."

"I heard you got beat up by a girl."

Damian turned his head sharply to look at her.

"What?" Jaden asked innocently. A megawatt smile was plastered on her face as she turned to meet his stare, but her body trembled with hatred. "You do remember what happened the last time you pulled this shit, don't you?"

"Relax. I'm here for the PR. That's it." His cocky voice matched his cocky smirk. He cinched his arm tighter around her waist and pulled her closer as he whispered, "Thanks for that, and thanks for this…"

"*One Hot Kitchen*, and one hot host!" he yelled to the crowd, and before Jaden knew what was happening, he'd scooped her body against his and planted a kiss that gave the cameras the shot they'd been waiting for. The more she struggled, the closer he held her to his chest, cementing the kiss and earning them a round of applause from the onlookers.

At last he removed his lips from hers. "Thanks for the front page, Jade."

It took every ounce of her energy to contain the sheer rage that pumped through her system, but on the red carpet in front of the press, what else could she do? Jaden just stood there, shocked and stunned, as she watched him slither away into *her* party, in *her* town.

He'd fucked her again. Thank God Ivan hadn't been here to witness that. But it didn't matter much. There'd been plenty of pictures and at least a few of them were probably up on the Internet already.

Gathering the sanity and dignity she had left, Jaden did her best to disappear. She headed for the bar, for Tasha, and perhaps a bottle of tequila.

Finding her friend, who was busy chatting away, she snatched the drink right out of her hand and slugged it down like a cold glass of water on a hot summer's day. But it wasn't. The liquid traced a scorching path down her throat and settled in her stomach.

"Good lord, Jaden, that was a glass of chilled tequila I was going to pour into shots. What's wrong with you?"

Trying to shake the sensation of burning alcohol from her throat, Jaden nodded in the direction of Damian, who was now smiling and nodding his way through the crowd.

"Holy shit!" Tasha looked from Damian to Jaden and back again. "Are you okay?"

"Let's just make it through this, okay?" All her excitement and hope for the evening had dissipated. Now she'd be reminded of her failings all night. "Fuck it. Give me another shot."

CHAPTER 15

"Sounds of Silence"

*S*ince he'd turned the corner and made the commitment to begin putting to rest the months of avoidance and turmoil he'd wrestled with post-Jaden, Ivan found that the sounds, smells, and tastes around him, which had been muted for months, had slowly begun to regain their luster. Take right now, for instance. The late-night air around him vibrated with electricity as he breathed in his surroundings: an A-list Miami Beach nightclub. After a long day at work he'd selected a spot in the middle of the lounge so he could absorb every bit of the energy. For the first time in months he felt clean of the addiction that had plagued him, and as he chatted with the waitresses, bartender, and fellow patrons sitting around him, he had no hidden agenda. The freak was silent as months of hidden sorrow and angst began to thaw and melt away.

Servers passed in a blur and two men in black suits began to rope off a reserved section across the room from where he sat. Ivan brought his glass of Jack on the rocks to his lips and sipped as he watched.

"Looks like they've got a big party coming in." A soft female voice spoke the exact words he'd been thinking.

His gaze followed the enchanting sound of her voice and there, three barstools away, sat a gorgeous blonde in a simple black dress.

She shook her head. "Probably nothing more than a pack of frat boys looking to spend daddy's money."

"Or a group of high-priced businessmen looking to spend their kids' college education," he added, smiling.

"You might get lucky," she said, returning his smile. "It could be a gaggle of bikini models fresh from a photo shoot."

"If only!" Ivan said with an honest to goodness laugh, half hoping the stranger was right.

She laughed with him and held up her wine glass as if to toast from across the distance. "I'll keep my fingers crossed for you."

Ivan raised his glass in her direction and kept his eyes trained on her as he took a drink.

She winked at him and turned back to face the bar. Much to his surprise, the freak was silent, but he was intrigued. There'd been no siren call, no overt flirting, and no licking of lips or beckoning looks. This was just a girl—albeit a stunning girl—who seemed to offer nothing but conversation and maybe a laugh or two. When she glanced back in his direction, he was still looking at her and smiling.

"Mind if I join you?" he asked, listening for the roar of the freak, but it never came.

She patted the leather barstool beside her and tipped her head. "Please do."

Ivan picked up his drink and walked over. In an effort to short-circuit the freak, should he decide to appear, he introduced himself. "I'm Ivan."

"Nice to meet you. I'm Elle."

Two drinks in, Ivan realized this was the first interesting conversation he'd had with a woman in months. She was funny, warm, and anything but the Miami Beach type he'd been accustomed to, and it was a nice change. He felt comfortable just being in the moment with her. It had been too long since he'd made an effort to talk to a woman he was interested in mentally, instead of just physically. Rather than being just a body, Elle was a face, she had a name, and he was thrilled to find himself making an effort to connect with her.

She had an accent he couldn't place. But he listened, enthralled, to her tales about her modeling career and travels across Europe and the United States. And his interest was really piqued when she admitted that modeling wasn't all it was cracked up to be, that she had ambition for something greater than the gloss. Ivan sat back and marveled. This was nothing like the small talk he'd occasionally endured with the women he'd frequented during the past few months—women who had too much to say about nothing.

"What do you want to do now? You're too young for retirement," he asked, fascinated by her eyes.

"Well, I'd have to say photography is my main love."

Interesting... This easy conversation, combined with the alcohol and the good vibrations, was the right kind of medicine. She was fun and unapologetically silly, and he genuinely enjoyed her company.

As they bantered back and forth, Ivan relished the return of the brilliant colors that only dirty, deviant sex had sparked for him the last few months. Even the pulse of the music felt stronger, more alive as it reverberated across his skin and down his chair, and the sounds of glasses clinking and cackles rising from the big spenders who'd just entered the bar sounded a bit more crisp. But they did little to deter his conversation with Elle. He was allowing himself to reclaim who and what he truly was, and it was invigorating.

Then, just as he raised his glass to his lips, someone bumped against the back of his chair. He lurched forward and spilled his drink over the rim. Elle gasped. The man mumbled a drunken apology, and Ivan blew it off as just some Miami Beach party boy—who smelled as if he'd had one too many. He shrugged and smiled at her, but instead of moving on, the man remained standing behind him, now bantering loudly with his buddy. Ignoring the drunken fools, Ivan tried to stay focused on his new friend, a woman he might actually be into.

"Damn, man, you should see what that ass looks like under that skirt. It's perfect."

"Fuck her ass! Look at her tits."

"Amazing, I know. Trust me."

The drunken banter grew louder, and it became virtually impossible to talk as the club grew more and more crowded around them. Elle smiled again, but turned her attention across the room to watch the dance floor for a while. Ivan followed her lead and decided on a little people watching of his own. But despite all efforts to ignore the men, he couldn't help but overhear the conversation unfolding behind him.

"What, did you fuck her?"

"It's a funny story."

"I knew you didn't."

"Now, hold on just a minute." The guy's voice grew irritated behind him.

"So, we're at this party, and she's drinking like it's going out of style. I catch on and start sending her drinks. She's sucking them down all night, and then she starts rambling to me about some boyfriend she has back home. One thing leads to another and—"

"Tell me you used the 'He'll never know' line."

"Damn right I did. Women eat that shit up."

The conversation behind him now commanded Ivan's full attention, so when the guy telling the story mentioned that woman with the perfect body was present in the room, and wearing a blue dress, he couldn't help but be intrigued. What man wouldn't be? The sound of the guy's voice grated on his nerves, but if she was half as gorgeous as he'd made her out to be, he had to at least have a look.

"Frankly, she was a little too easy."

"So did you fuck her?"

Like an overly dramatic *telenovela* on Spanish TV, Ivan was drawn in by the ridiculous story line and cheesy one-liners he heard. He had to know how it ended for his own amusement.

"I finally convince her to leave the event, and by that point I'd gotten her drunk enough to let me drive her home—to my house, of course. As we're driving, I start trailing my finger up her leg, dipping it under skirt. Getting her all worked up, you know. I could tell she'd already made up her mind at the party, so I was just playing with her. And the second I pull in the driveway—before we even get out of the goddamn car—she literally jumps across the seat and starts grinding into my lap and sticking her tongue down my throat."

Elle leaned over and placed a hand on his arm. "I have to run to the ladies' room," she told him. "Will you be here when I get back?"

"Absolutely," he said, nodding. "Maybe by then they'll be gone and we'll be able to hear each other again!"

She smiled and disappeared, leaving him free to focus on the train wreck of a conversation behind him.

"You better have fucked her proper."

"Here's the fucking thing. We get inside, barely, and I get her down to her bra and panties in sixty seconds flat. Drunk women are so easy. And she's hot, trust me. Lean legs, toned stomach, and an ass to die for—a really sporty-looking fuck. So we start making out again real hardcore, and I think I said or called her something I shouldn't have, because out of nowhere she just fucking stopped with this blank look on her face and broke down crying."

"Ouch."

"I love my boyfriend...I can't believe I'm doing this," the drunk whined in a high-pitched voice. "You know, the typical shit that falls out of a woman's mouth when she's had too much."

"So, she wasn't kidding about the boyfriend, eh?"

"Yeah, he's some asshole who lives here in Miami, actually. Seems like a real dickhead."

Now thoroughly intrigued, Ivan took pity on the guy in the story. Unfortunately, he could totally relate. *Poor guy must have shitty taste in women, but I gotta see this girl.* He turned and cased the room for the heartless bitch with a killer body in the blue dress. His eyes moved over dancing party-goers and desperate hopefuls, but nowhere was there a blue dress hiding the promise of physical perfection. Then his eyes fell on a once-vacant table that had now been filled by the private party. The dress wasn't blue, though. It was teal.

The curve of her hip was one he knew well. He'd gripped it many times before. He knew the feel of the V that formed at the top of her breasts. He'd often laid his face against her soft skin as he fell asleep in her arms. And he knew firsthand the boyfriend in this romantic tragedy who had shitty taste in women. It was him.

CHAPTER 16

"Freak on a Leash"

"She was so drunk, the bitch ended up passing out. I got her good in the morning though. Told her we fucked." A snorting laugh followed this revelation.

"You didn't!"

"Yeah, I did. Handle your fucking liquor, slut. She learned a lesson from it too. She and her boyfriend broke up, and of course I was the bad guy. But screw her—she wasted my night."

Ivan stared dead ahead at the girl he'd thought he'd known as he listened to the evidence of his romantic homicide being confessed. And the confession was quite different than he'd imagined. Damian Gris's heartless claims of victory and conquest over someone Ivan held so dear shot rage through his body.

Each word, each claim, each twisted truth deepened the veil of red forming over his eyes, and within moments, Ivan had lost the battle with his inner beast. The freak he'd subdued just days ago was now off the leash. This time anger had wound the freak into a maddening frenzy of fury, rather than lust. An orgasm of rage heightened his senses and made clear his direction.

Every moment of despair Ivan had felt in the past six months filled his mind at once—the look on Jaden's face the night she'd broken him, days and nights of crushing emotional pain, and the nameless faces of the women who'd served as his sexual painkillers. The wreck his life had been saddened him, and it was all authored by *him* and his manipulation of *her*.

But after a moment, one emotion rose above the swirling anger and angst: pity. He felt sorrow that the beautiful person he'd loved so dearly had been taken advantage of by this evil, empty creature standing behind him. Inebriation was no excuse for unfaithfulness, whether consummated or not, but the malicious intent that had instigated the situation was intolerable.

Damian had ruined what he had with Jaden for no real reason at all—just a drunken haze of frat boy antics and perverse mind games. How fucking *dare* he?

Anger, confusion, and pity ripped through Ivan like an emotional tornado, leaving nothing solid in their path except for a voice. Above the noise came the voice that had counseled him on the beach the morning after his heart was broken, the voice that had urged him to numb his mental anguish with hard work and even harder fucking, and the voice that now demanded he should have retribution for all that had been lost—for himself and for Jaden. The freak had returned. And he was pissed.

Without hesitation Ivan stood, feeling the frenzy of hormones and emotions that energized his body, readying him for confrontation. He turned to look at the man who had wronged his right, who had deliberately, and without care, ruined his life and his one true chance at happiness: Damian Gris. The little faux French fucker deserved at the very least to have his teeth kicked in, the freak advised as Ivan's muscles swelled. Sounds and sights appeared brighter and louder than they had in months, and finally his desire and the freak's were the same: retribution.

"So did you ever figure out what flipped her out?" Damian's friend inquired, still absorbed by the story.

"Damned if I know. One minute we're standing there kissing, and the next minute she's in hysterics. All I did was called her something stupid like girly, or baby, or—"

"Baby girl?" Ivan offered, abruptly entering their conversation. He offered a wide, menacing grin as the pathetic excuse for a human turned to identify who had spoken.

"Can I help you with something?" Damian's friend inquired.

Not even sparing the guy a glance, Ivan raised his hand to silence him. His eyes, which felt as if they were beaming fire, locked on Damian's icy blues. In an instant he had mirrored Ivan's aggressive stance.

"Dude, why don't you just piss off and leave us the fuck alone?" his friend suggested.

Not letting his focus falter for one second, Ivan refused to acknowledge the guy. Toe to toe, he faced the demon.

"This is the cocksucker I was telling you about," Damian said with a laugh, his eyes widening in recognition. "Jaden's *ex* boyfriend."

As if the two men exuded some sort of testosterone-driven beacon, a small group began to form around them, the crowd sensing something was escalating.

"You know, you should thank me," Damian sneered. "I saved you from getting screwed over later on. Little bitches like that always fuck us over in the end."

Was that Damian's problem? Had he fallen in love only to get his heart crushed? Was this what happened when the freak took full control of the man? He became a womanizing, egotistical bastard like Damian Gris?

Ivan just shook his head. *Pathetic.* Damian didn't deserve a verbal response, nor did he deserve a fist, but he certainly didn't deserve to walk out of this place without learning a life lesson.

The freak screamed again, and Ivan lunged forward, a jolt of excitement surging through him as he prepared to unleash upon Damian exactly what a creature of his magnitude deserved: the back of his hand.

Every muscle in Ivan's shoulder flexed as the back of his hand extended toward the side of Damian's pretty-boy face. As flesh met flesh, Ivan returned a little of the embarrassment, pain, sorrow, and loathing he'd endured courtesy of Damian. The adrenaline rush and sting in his hand were more gratifying than every sexual encounter he'd had in the last six months added up and multiplied by ten. The freak's demand for retribution matched his thirst for climax, and they collaborated in a fantastic moment of having avenged what was lost. The demon had been vanquished, and Ivan had reclaimed a piece of his pride.

Caught off guard, Damian lost his balance and crashed back into the bar, knocking his friend over in the process. He looked up at the man who'd just backhanded him with hatred smoldering in the depths of his eyes. A collective snicker rippled through the crowd of bystanders.

"Are you done here, Ivan?" the bouncer called from behind the onlookers.

Snapping out of his fury, Ivan smiled at the bouncer before turning his attention back to Damian, who remained on the floor. It seemed he did not care to tango — not tonight, not ever.

Ivan leaned down, his voice low and menacing. "How did that taste, asshole?"

Damian just stared back, gasping like a fish out of water.

"Yeah, I figured as much," Ivan scoffed. He motioned to the bouncer. "Get these clowns outta here, would you?"

In one rough motion, and with little regard for their wellbeing, the security guard parted the crowd and grabbed each of the men by their shirts. He dragged them to their feet and toward the door.

A wave of giggles and murmuring followed them out, but after a few moments, with no more to see, the crowd dispersed. Ivan took a deep breath and felt a momentary lightness. The weight of this burden had finally been lifted from his shoulders, but he wasn't done. The freak was free, and it was time to right so many, many wrongs.

Despite the release he'd relished after confronting Damian, he could already feel the tension returning. So now the freak turned his head toward her. He looked over the heads of the crowd, many of them still conversing about the bitch slap that had sent a TV star flying, and found the girl in the teal dress. Suddenly every other woman in the club faded away. The freak had made his choice. Even he wanted Jaden.

She and Tasha sat side by side, giggling and sipping martinis, and the veil fell over Ivan's eyes once more. Making the same beeline he'd made in Bianca what seemed like a million lifetimes ago, he darted through the crowd and across the dance floor. As he approached, a second burly security guard nodded and stepped aside.

"Hey, Doc," the man greeted him as he granted access to the roped-off area.

"Hey, Sam," Ivan replied as he pushed past the crowd lingering to get a better look at the beautiful people behind the ropes.

More than a few heads turned as he crossed the room, but the girl who sat with her back to him—the one and only person Ivan wanted to notice him—remained oblivious. As he came to stand next to her, he held his breath. Finally sensing his presence, Jaden turned in her seat to face him. Her eyes, as green as emeralds in the mid-day sun, locked with his for the first time in what seemed like an eternity. How long had it been since her words had broken him? He could tell by her face that those same words now echoed in both their ears.

A two-second visual conversation was all he needed. Emotions rushed through him—hate, love, anger, lust, disdain, sorrow, pity, envy—until he had no idea what he felt. But pinpointing his feelings didn't matter. He was drawn to her presence, and he knew from experience that the freak was not about to turn back now. He didn't care about the anger, he didn't care about the confusion, and he didn't care about the pity. All he cared about was reclaiming what had been stolen. What tomorrow brought was insignificant. Tonight she would be his, and that's all that mattered.

Silently, he extended his hand to her. Wordlessly, she accepted.

The feel of her skin against his sent a flash of energy though his body. He prepared himself for a night of passion that wasn't spoken but screamed.

CHAPTER 17
"Crazy Bitch"

Ivan took Jaden's hand and led her back through the dance floor and around the bar, blindly pushing past anything between them and the back exit of the club. They crashed through the doors and out into a secluded, dimly lit alley, hidden by the small hours of a muggy Miami Beach night.

"Ivan, I am so — " Jaden began to speak the second they stepped outside, but he pressed her into the wall, pinning her to the brick with his forearms and cutting off an unfinished apology that wouldn't do either of them justice.

He crushed his lips to hers and pushed his arousal against her thigh as he raised her leg and placed it around his waist. She tasted just as sweet as she always had. The essence of dry martinis and salt air lingered in her mouth, and he forced his tongue farther to drink it in.

A cacophony of passionate gasps and moans mingled with the sounds of passing traffic as they explored once familiar, yet now foreign grounds. Dropping his mouth to the skin behind her ear, Ivan sucked and nipped a trail of kisses down her neck and across her shoulder until he found the curve he knew all too well, the V between her breasts. The familiar fragrance of lavender and coconut triggered an indescribable reaction, one he hadn't felt in so long. This was what he craved: her touch and her smell.

His hands trailed over her body and ravished her breasts. He raised her other leg, hooking it around his body and pinning her harder against the wall. His cock, now at full attention, pressed more urgently into her thigh.

He ground into her, and Jaden matched his movements, swaying her hips from side to side and eliciting a guttural moan from deep within his chest. This was the ultimate fix. This was his cure. She was it. She was his.

Jaden grabbed a fistful of his hair and yanked his head back, forcing him to look at her as she seemed to search for something he wasn't communicating. Her breath heavy and unsteady, she ran gentle fingers across his face and jaw. Ivan brought his hand around to the back of her neck and tilted her head, his teeth ripping at her bottom lip. Her body responded as it always had, and she clutched his hair with both hands.

Releasing her bottom lip from his teeth, he held her face between his hands, studying her face, her reaction as he held her against the bricks with his body. She was every bit as beautiful as he remembered, but he could not look at her now without feeling the pain of having been ripped in two. But this was not the time for feelings. He looked her up and down and marveled at her beauty as the freak within trembled in excitement. *Satisfaction.*

Jaden tried to pull back and speak between kisses, but he kept cutting her off. He kissed her hard as he yanked the teal dress up around her waist, exposing her lacy, black panties, moist with intent. He watched her reaction as his fingers pushed aside the fabric and came to rest between her legs. He could feel the wetness mounting, her body readying itself for him.

"Ivan," she mumbled between gasping breaths, but he silenced her again with his touch.

He plunged two fingers into her, and she squirmed beneath him. The feel of her warmth illuminated the dim alley in a medley of sounds and colors. Faster and faster he worked his fingers in and out of her and reveled in the sensation of power. He held her against the wall and had his way with her, smiling as she writhed and bit her lip in ecstasy.

He felt her legs begin to tremble as they always did when she was ready to come, and he picked up the pace, curling his fingers inside her to rake against the sweet spot. Her mouth dropped open as she clamped around his fingers and convulsed with orgasm, but he didn't stop. Instead, he continued to thrust his fingers into her, the palm of his hand rubbing against her clit with every stroke, and driving her straight into another orgasm.

As Jaden felt the last orgasmic tremors subside, Ivan withdrew his fingers from her body and released her. He backed away to lean against the opposite wall. She was taken aback by the feral glint in his eyes, but now was not the time or place to analyze anything. She wanted him to be in her.

She closed the gap between them and pressed her body against his. But he didn't respond, not the way he usually would. His hands were knotted in his hair, his eyes raised to the sky above them. It was clear he wasn't interested in talking, but at that moment neither was she. Moving into hardcore seduction mode, she brushed her breasts against him. He moaned, but when she tried to kiss him, he dodged her lips and offered his neck to her. She took what he gave. As she bit his neck, she reached between them and ran her hand across his hard cock, still tucked away. When she pulled back to look at his face, his eyes were closed and a tense wrinkle knit across his brow. She unzipped his pants and heard him hiss as she took him in her hand. She stroked the length of him once, twice, and on the third pull, his eyes flew open and locked on hers.

Ivan's breathing was heavy but controlled as she continued to manipulate him. Then finally, he ran his hands along the sides of her neck and tangled them in her hair. He studied her as he held her face in his hands, then pulled her roughly to his lips and moaned loudly in her mouth before he broke away.

Jaden quickly found him again and moved her hand in a steady motion while she rubbed her body against his. His stomach flexed and twitched with every stroke, and as she watched, his eyes rolled back in his head and the veins and muscles in his neck strained under the intensity.

"Wait," he said sharply, glancing over his shoulder.

She did as he asked but didn't back away or let go. Ivan reached between them and moved himself out of her grip with a bit of a groan. He stepped back and zipped up his pants.

Jaden smoothed her dress, and when they both looked somewhat presentable, she took his hand and led him to the street. "Follow me."

Cars sped past in a blur as they stood on the sidewalk. Jaden signaled for a taxi. When at last they were able to hail one, they fell into the backseat.

"Where to?" the taxi driver asked.

Jaden could feel Ivan's stare. Her place was farther, but she was making the decisions, at least for the moment. She gave him her address and the car raced toward her apartment. Silence settled over the backseat, and Jaden had no idea what to say—or if she should even speak. It had been six months since Ivan had even really acknowledged she existed, and what happened in the alleyway had certainly taken her by surprise. So much needed to be said, and yet there were no words.

She looked over at him sitting beside her and watched the lights from passing stores and streetlights dance across his face. The illumination accented his elegant features, and she longed to lean over and kiss him. But he didn't hold her hand or snuggle up beside her. Instead, he sat wordless and motionless, a stranger of sorts. He offered her no more than the occasional casual glance, wearing a poker face she'd never seen and couldn't read. It intrigued her sexually but worried her all the same.

It was undoubtedly him, but he was different, and not just because he'd let his hair grow out and grown a beard. There was a hardened edge to him now. Jaden stared at him as they rode in silence. She drew her hand to her swollen and tender lips, remembering the feel of his mouth on hers and the tickle of his whiskers against her cheeks. Her eyes drifted from the top of his head, past the cowlick in his hairline to his beautiful profile, the small scar above his left eyebrow, and the curve of his ear. Her hands were desperate to touch him. And yet she didn't dare.

What did this mean? Why had he done this? Did he want her back? Did he forgive her, or had her actions changed him, and changed them, forever? But the answers didn't really matter. She needed him, and she wanted this—whatever *this* was. No matter the consequences, she'd pay them just to have him back, even if for only a moment in time.

"You can stop here," she called to the driver and threw a ten-dollar bill onto the front seat. Without a word, she reached for Ivan's hand and pulled him from the cab.

CHAPTER 18

"Hold On"

As the elevator ascended, Jaden's mind raced. What did this mean? Did she have the right to be hopeful after what she'd done to him? To them? God, she hoped so.

In the light now, she studied him more carefully than the dim alley and taxi had allowed. When her focus shifted from his sharp jaw and lips to his eyes, slightly obscured by the errant strands of hair that hung over his face, she found him staring back at her. He seemed to look into her soul in a way he'd never done before. Or maybe she'd just forgotten. It was as if he searched for the answer to a question that hadn't been asked out loud.

The tension between them grew ever thicker, and their silence more and more awkward. But what should you say to a man who'd just had his way with you against a damp brick wall after you refused his proposal months ago? "I'm sorry" just didn't seem like enough. "I'll do whatever it takes" was a start, but based on the way he looked at her from across the elevator, she suspected he already knew that. The question was: Would it be enough?

Goose bumps pricked at her skin, and she shivered with anticipation as his lips curled into a seductive smile. She watched his face as he studied her. She could tell he was in to this, but was he in to *her*? That was harder to say. Jaden bit her lip and waited for his reaction, which was pretty much instantaneous. He tried to conceal his mounting...*interest*...by shifting his stance, but she knew him too well. She smiled, feeling more confident, but then the heavy-lidded gaze he turned on her went dark, sexy, and dangerously raw—not like the Ivan she remembered at all. She could feel her heart beating in her throat. Evidently a little danger and a whole lot of sexy was one hell of a turn on for her. Good thing too, because the shadow that darkened his eyes seemed to be setting the mood for the evening.

With a ping, the doors to the elevator slid open, but neither of them moved, their eyes locked in a lusty stare. The old Ivan would have guided her out of the elevator with his hand at the small of her back or by taking her hand in his. However, after a moment, this new Ivan gestured to the open door and tipped his head toward the corridor with a smile.

Jaden grabbed his hand as she passed, towing him out of the elevator behind her. She tried to steady her breathing as she walked down the hall. If she hadn't been able to feel the warmth of his hand in hers, she might have been convinced this was all a dream. And even so, if she glanced over her shoulder or closed her eyes too tightly, she wondered if he might disappear as he had so many times in her fantasies. She dared a look behind her. He was here now, and she was going to make tonight amazing for as long as he wanted. And after that, if he ever let her speak, she'd fall at his feet, repentant for her sins, and hope he believed there was something between them to salvage. For her, there was no doubt.

Resigned to whatever lay ahead, she gripped his hand tighter and picked up the pace. When Jaden stalled at the door, fumbling for the key, he grasped her waist, warming her hip bones with grip that screamed eroticism and need. Her body reacted immediately as a hint of the old Ivan rushed through her. His closeness behind her made it impossible to fit the damn key into the lock. The feel of his breath on the back of her neck was intensified by his beard as it raked across her spine. She arched her back and pushed her ass into his crotch, relishing the hardness that pressed back against her.

Finally managing the lock, she flung the door open and the two plunged inside. She turned in his arms and met his eyes, silently pleading for what her mind, body, and soul craved. Without words she grasped his shirt, pulling him into her darkened apartment and back into her life—at least for tonight. She would take it. She'd take anything he offered.

Ivan gathered her roughly in his arms and searched her face with that unfamiliar gaze. He kicked up his foot and slammed the door behind them, then pulled her close to kiss her hard. Jaden dropped her bag and keys at their feet and put everything she had into kissing him back. Her relentlessness matched his aggression. She guided him toward her bedroom as they ripped at each other's clothing like wild beasts. She sent buttons flying as she exposed his chest and stomach. Ivan grasped her waist and threw her onto the bed in a fury of passion and want.

In the pale moonlight she watched as he pulled his tattered shirt from his body and threw it to the floor beside him. He slid his hands up the sides of her legs, beneath the hem of her dress, and grasped her lacy panties, ripping them from her body. He looked down on her, breathing heavily, as if he were considering something. Jaden searched his face, quietly trying to reach the part of him that might still love her — the soft part of his heart that might bring him back. But all she could discern was carnal desire staring back at her, and she couldn't help but lick her lips in response. As Ivan bent down, she braced herself for what was sure to be pure ecstasy. He grabbed her hips roughly and dragged her ass toward him, forcing her dress up around her waist as she moved across the bed, spreading herself open for him.

She arched her back as she felt his hot breath wash over her damp pussy. Running her fingers through his hair, she shuddered as his tongue began exploring her. She couldn't help but moan aloud as he tongued her further and further into a frenzy, pulling begging whimpers of *fuck me* and *love me* from her.

As he slid a finger into her, Jaden nearly came at just the thought of him fucking her. When he slid the second one in, she did. Exploding around his fingers and tongue, she rocked her body back and forth. *God, this is it* she thought as she ground her pussy against his bristled face and pulled at his long hair. She'd dreamed of being back in his embrace for so long, and she was finally there, her hips held in place as his mouth coaxed her to climax. She held back tears as her orgasm subsided and her body slowed its rhythm. Returning to his feet, Ivan tossed his long, dark hair away from his face.

He looked down at her once again as he unbuttoned his pants. They dropped to the floor, along with his briefs. His dick stood fully erect, and Jaden marveled at the authority and demand that radiated from his body. Offering herself in the best way she knew how, she rolled onto her stomach and presented her ass to him. It was his. And only his.

As Jaden adjusted her position, clearly offering herself to him, Ivan felt a rush of entitlement. This was his redemption. This was his sexual justice. Except…

He knelt and reached into his pants pocket for a condom. No matter how much he needed this, there were rules. Tearing it open with his teeth, he made quick work of rolling it over his shaft. The smell of sex filled his nostrils as lust soaked his brain. He grabbed her hips and positioned his cock at the entrance of this long, lost secret that he loved so much. *Mine.*

Running his tongue along his beard, he savored the flavor she'd left on him — the definition of sex. Focusing his attention, Ivan steadied himself with his firm grasp on her hips. He repositioned his hands and held her tightly against him. He closed his eyes, and with a final push he entered a world that soothed his spirit, sedated his tortured mind, and brought him untainted pleasure for the first time in ages. The sensations were blinding, deafening, and overwhelming as he entered her over and over again, pushing deeper with every thrust. More, harder, farther, the freak, his body, and his own soul demanded as his fingers encircled her waist, pulling her harder and faster into his strokes. His body rejoiced as it fucked itself to contentment, and his mind celebrated being set free from the prison that had held it these past months.

"Ahh, ahh, ahh, ahh, Ivan!"

He drank in the sounds as she writhed under his dick. He fucked her hard like only he knew how to do. Their bodies fell into a rhythm that no class could teach. She rebounded her ass in perfect time to his upward strokes. But he needed to feel her even more. He smacked her ass, eliciting a sound that filled the room, followed by her gasp of pleasure. He knew he was in control, and he — and the freak — loved it.

Releasing his iron-clad grip on her waist, he pulled out of her and tugged at the zipper of her dress. He yanked the soft fabric from her body, enjoying the sound of Jaden's gasp and her low moan of excitement. He flipped her over and tackled her on the bed, falling against her naked body and indulging in the warmth that now surrounded him. He couldn't see her smile, but he felt it as his lips closed on hers. Her lips were intoxicating—how long had it been since his lips had felt any other's, let alone hers?— and he relished them for a moment before raising the backs of her knees to rest on his shoulders.

Stealing one final taste of her lips, he plunged into her wetness. An explosion of color burst through the darkness of the room as he penetrated her more deeply than he ever thought he could. He felt her writhe under his force. As he continued to fuck her relentlessly, his body trembled and he climbed to the highest sexual peak he could imagine. Every sense heightened as if this were a drug which was laced with something he'd never tasted before. He wanted more, and she seemed perfectly willing to give it.

Whatever lay ahead for them, if anything at all, he'd earned this after the last six months of torture she'd put him through. Grabbing her wrists, he pulled her up into a curled ball of heat and sweat as his rhythm in and out of her quickened along with their breathing. Although he couldn't see her eyes in the darkness, when she rolled her neck back for a deep groan, he glimpsed them for a moment. They looked back at him with the same ferocity as he knew his burned into her. But he was in charge now. This was his moment. His climax.

Harder and faster his cock plunged in and out as he changed his angle with each penetration. He hit every inch of her core with menacing delight. Their breaths grew unified as each inhale brought a moment of relief only to be followed by an exhale of pleasure and pain. His nostrils filled with the scent he'd longed for on so many long, lonely nights in his bed. The scent of pure, lavender-and-coconut-laced sex tantalized him, fueling a progression that, once it had begun, screamed through his body. His toes curled and his spine began its telltale loosening in preparation for an orgasm that was seconds around the corner.

The sensation of Jaden trying to free her hands to cope with her orgasm, which now tightened around his cock, was the tipping point—the beginning of the end of a six-month sabbatical from the most beautiful of nirvanas. Tightening his grip around her wrists he pulled his ass high in the air and then slammed himself back down into her. The feeling was magical. Again he brought his ass up only to drive his cock further into her. *Almost.* His body taunted him with a glimpse of pure heaven.

His next thrust plunged him into complete bliss, and he felt as if bright lights exploded around him and in him. This encounter had taken him higher than he'd ever been in his life. As his body trembled inside her, he collapsed onto her and held her tight. She clamped her knees around his shoulders and took all of him she could. The seven seconds of perfection this act provided meant the satisfaction he'd longed for.

He nestled his head in the crook of her neck and held on to her wrists, keeping the feeling for as long as he could. This moment was perfect: no pain, no fear, no confusion or questions. He wished he could freeze time and never leave.

As the sensation diminished, so did the guard he'd meticulously maintained to protect himself. He could feel his heart flickering to life. *Perhaps...*He felt the pang of pity shove aside the anger and sorrow and disappointment he'd felt for so long. An encounter that had started in an alley as the freak's ultimate conquest, the sweetest revenge, had evolved into...the possibility of something more. Perhaps this woman could be his future, his destiny, after all.

CHAPTER 19

"If You Leave"

Ivan released Jaden's wrists and felt the blood rush back into his fingers. Gentle now, he coaxed her legs from over his shoulders and helped her uncoil. He smiled as she hummed in pleasure—or maybe it was sadness?—as he shifted his hips and the last bit of her heaven slid away from him. He deftly removed the condom and tossed it to the floor. It was a burden he didn't want to acknowledge.

He crawled over to lie beside her on the bed, cloaked in darkness. Neither of them spoke a word as their lust dissipated into an afterglow that seemed to engulf them both. Unlike the distance he'd previously maintained, Ivan now sought to continue their connection and enjoy the moment. He slowly traced his finger up from the top of her naked thigh, past her hip, across her stomach and to her nipple, which he circled softly. His dissipated fury had left him awash in a rush of endorphins.

From time to time he sensed that Jaden was on the verge of saying something, but she remained quiet. Hastened breaths would hint at an impending exclamation, but then dissolve into a sigh as she indulged in the feeling of his touch.

Moments turned to minutes and minutes to hours as the two lay in silence. Ivan's mind roved in search of some sort of explanation for the evening, and he guessed Jaden was trying to make sense of it as well. More importantly, he wondered what was to come. But he couldn't quite bring himself to spoil this moment. He didn't know when, or if, the next one might come.

He marveled at how connected they'd once been and realized he didn't know much about her life now at all. But she seemed successful in a world she'd always wanted to be in. He was happy for that. And he knew she was single because people always told him her situation, even though he never asked. But he also couldn't deny the occasional Google recon when times felt especially tough.

After hearing Damian's story at the bar and sharing the last several hours with her, his mind—and certainly his body—had begun hinting at the future. And now, for the first time, he began to think it might be possible. He'd spent so long shutting himself off from everything that didn't go his way, trying to eliminate pain, but perhaps this was something worth repairing. Her love was worth the fall, and it always had been.

His soft caresses turned into a massage, which caused her body to melt under his touch as it had so many times before. How many times had he massaged her to sleep after a night of passion? He savored every sensation and smell around him at this moment. He believed it was something, much like their time spent in the cabin and their moment in the vineyard, that would live in his soul forever.

Ivan gently rolled Jaden away from him onto her side and slid closer, resting her body on his where it fit so perfectly. He propped himself up on one elbow and gathered all of her hair in his hands, raking his fingers through the heavy, tumbling mass and dropping his lips to her neck. He indulged in his most favorite scent in the world. *Jaden.* She nestled against him and sighed when he pushed her hair aside and continued her massage as the sun began to rise, slowly illuminating her bedroom and their bodies. After some time, the masterpiece of a night of unbridled emotions dissolved completely, and they lay open and exposed in the light of day. It was magnificent.

Her ebony hair fanned across the white bedspread like a stenciled work of art. He watched her chest rise and fall with every precious breath. She was thinner now, her ribs more prominent, but her skin was still the perfect shade of tan, and he couldn't help but steal a taste. He kissed her shoulder and reeled at the salt on her flesh. It was delicious. His fingers worked the small of her back as he continued to take her in. He needed her. And he needed to tell her.

"Jaden," he called softly.

No response.

"Jaden?"

Still nothing.

Listening for a moment, he heard the sounds of her breath, indicating a deep sleep he knew all too well. Smiling, he contemplated his next move. Being able to lie there and enjoy having her in his arms again seemed like a great idea, but he knew she'd be out for hours. Even after further indulgence, he'd be ready to move before she was.

When he finally grew so restless he feared he'd wake her, he decided breakfast in bed would be a good way to begin the conversation he now believed he wanted to have. This mess with Damian was over. It had been over for a long time, really. And if anything remained, he'd finished it last night—with him and with her. A smile flickered across his face, and, careful not to wake her, he maneuvered his way out of bed. He couldn't help but glance back to watch her sleep. It was beautiful.

After he found his clothes, he silently gathered the evidence of carnal relations and slipped into the bathroom. He tossed the condom in the garbage and went to work cleaning himself up. He turned the water on, then cupped his hands under it and splashed it on his face.

As the cold water streamed down his cheeks, he looked in the mirror and saw a little black patchwork bear looking back at him. The sight nearly brought him to his knees. In a rush he remembered every instant, every memory attached to that bear, which told the tale of true love. He was so glad to see it. He began to dress and had to laugh when he pulled on his shirt and realized there was only one surviving button. *Some things never change.*

Once he had everything he thought he'd come in with back on, he tiptoed back into the bedroom. He stole another glimpse to confirm she was still asleep, and then crept out of the apartment to find breakfast. He left the door unlocked behind him so he could be sure to surprise her upon his return.

He went down the elevator, through the lobby, and out the door—he hadn't paid much attention when the cab had dropped them off in the dark, but now that he had his bearings, he had to laugh. Jaden's building was right next to his. *Damn convenient.* She'd been in his 'hood this whole time, and he'd never known—she'd probably never known. He pulled the flyaway tails of his shirt around him and trotted over to the fresh juice place just a couple doors down. He wanted it to be perfect. Exhaling an out-of-breath order for two juices and various yogurt, fruit, and granola combinations, Ivan then found a seat to contemplate what he *really* wanted. Should he attempt to move cautiously? Start slowly again? Should he jump right back into it? He sighed. After six months of *not* thinking about it, suddenly everything came in a rush.

Back and forth he went until his eyes came to rest on an image his mind couldn't fathom. Staring back at him from the morning paper, which was scattered across an adjacent table, were two people he recognized: one wore a teal dress, and she was wrapped in a devil's embrace, his lips ravishing hers. Ivan didn't even have to read the headline, but the large black letters spelled it out for him anyway: *Jaden Thorne and Damian Gris Make for One Hot Event.*

"Fuck me," escaped him, and an elderly couple sitting nearby looked over.

Done. It's done. He couldn't possibly open himself to this kind of pain anymore. The picture mocked him from the table, display-ing itself for everyone in Miami — all his friends and associates and colleagues — to see. Maybe she hadn't chosen Damian, maybe he'd manipulated her, but she'd certainly chosen fame at any cost — and that was somehow worse. Why else would she fake a relationship with him for the cameras? Someone she loathed, and with quite good reason — why wasn't she strong enough to say no?

It just wasn't worth getting back into it, because evidently the mess with Damian was far from over. One way or another, she would con-tinue to make this decision, become anyone she needed to be, and continue to screw him, over and over again. What would happen the next time she felt overwhelmed or they had a fight? Maybe next time her conscience wouldn't be strong enough to stop her. Maybe she hadn't really loved him at all, at least not the way he'd thought she did.

"Ivan!" His order was ready.

Feeling sick to his stomach, he approached the counter, expres-sionless and devoid of any hope. In the time it took for the kid to make two juices, the earth had tilted on its axis and knocked him off his feet. Again.

"You okay?"

"Yeah. You have a pen?"

"Yep." The clerk reached into the pocket of his ridiculous yellow outfit.

"Can I get one of these?" Ivan motioned to the newspaper.

"Sure, man. Just take one. No one buys them anyway."

"Thanks, boss."

Ivan picked up his order, his evidence, the pen, and a stack of napkins and returned to his seat to plot the course for his future. He wrote, pouring his heart onto the paper in black ink. When he'd finished he read and reread what he'd written before gathering his things and returning to her apartment. Each step felt as if he had irons tethered around his ankles.

Just at the other side of her door, he stalled out and stood staring at the numbers fastened to it: 1218. He prayed she was still asleep and he could slip in without her knowing. Slowly he turned the unlocked knob and pushed the door open. He poked his head in to check. He could hear nothing. Finally he crept in and tiptoed to the bedroom, only to find the demon in an angel's skin still sound asleep.

He watched her for a time, asking himself over and over if this was what he wanted to do. But the headline ran through his head, and he knew it was the smart play, the self-preserving play. He was finished being a fool. What they'd once had, the person he'd thought she'd been, was gone.

Ivan stole into the bathroom, grabbed the token of a young love lost, and returned to her bedroom. He set up the breakfast he'd meant to share on the dresser near her bed and placed the bear next to it, on top of the newspaper and holding a pile of paper napkins. Then he took a final look at her, made a final gut check, and left the apartment.

He told himself he was going back to a life he was now free to live, free to find a way to enjoy. His burden had been lifted.

CHAPTER 20

"Waiting for the End"

As rays of sun warmed her skin, Jaden's mind powered on before her eyes or the rest of her body followed. She smiled as the night rushed back to her, and she relived its passion in seconds. The incredible ache in all the right places, along with the tender spots on her hips and wrists that she knew Ivan's hands had marked, elicited another grin. Her fingers traced her hip, and she breathed out a soft laugh. Yep, he'd left his mark. He may as well have spelled out, *IVAN WAS HERE.* She stretched and flexed her body, enjoying every twinge as she twisted in the sheets. Her whole body throbbed in the aftermath of pleasure.

Her body also registered the fact that there was no arm draped over her before her brain did. No sweaty torso tucked in behind her. No breath danced across the back of her neck. A siren of alarm began to whine in her body, but nothing from the night before had hinted she'd be waking up alone this morning.

As her eyes opened and caught up to the rest of her body, they went in search of answers. She rolled over to find the answer staring back at her with black button eyes. Noting the breakfast for two, she was eager to see what good news BoBo had to deliver this time. She bounced across the room to the dresser in search of one of Ivan's infamous notes. "Thank you, BoBo," she mused aloud as she snagged the napkins.

Still naked, she made herself comfortable with the pillows and linens all piled up in the middle of the bed and began to read.

Jaden,

Last night was amazing. I'd forgotten what it was like to feel such intense chemistry and unspoken connection with another person's soul. If I'd slept at all it would have been a waste of such a perfect moment. But I didn't sleep, and instead I dreamed of a destiny I thought I'd lost.

Overwhelmed with the words, Jaden smiled as she continued to the next napkin.

I've always viewed love and its progression as an education. You learn from your failures and grow with successes. Many of these lessons are hard learned, but the result can be pure magic that makes every tear shed worth it. I can say without a doubt that the love we shared has been my greatest educator. It has taught me to understand what I need in my life to truly be happy. But it has also shown me what I can't have in order to do so.

She paused at the sudden turn and felt foreboding begin to build within her. Yet she continued.

Last night, with you, my everything was distilled into a singular magical symphony of beauty and perfection. But this morning served me with an unwanted lesson in my continued education. A lesson in dreams versus reality. Fate versus hope. Business versus pleasure.

The foreboding turned to queasiness, and Jaden dropped the napkin to her lap—not daring to read any more. She looked back to the bear that had once delivered such a beautiful message, but who now seemed to have betrayed her. She forced herself to continue.

As you fell asleep under my touch, I imagined a life where the mistakes of the past held no bearing on the prosperity of the future. One where love would find a way, like in a fairy tale. But this enthusiasm, anchored only by a breath of possibility, has been tainted by an ugly realization...a single image that warns of countless future risks and pitfalls.

What the hell is he talking about? Jaden now felt a flush of anger and confusion. She looked back to the bear as if to ask for an explanation. It was then she noticed that BoBo and the breakfast were not the only new items on her dresser. Under him sat a folded newspaper. In a flood of panic she snatched it, toppling the bear to its side. She quickly placed him back upright, feeling foolish for believing she needed to.

As she scanned the paper, anger, embarrassment, and sorrow flooded her entire body, replacing the warmth she'd awoken with.

"Oh my God," she gasped. The sight of that bastard all over her was sickening. But nauseated or not, she forced herself to skim the article.

> JADEN THORNE, formerly linked to Dr. Ivan Rusilko as half of last year's gorgeous Miami Beach power couple, cozies up to her recently departed *One Hot Kitchen* co-host, Damian Gris. Gris is set to star in the new series *What a Man Wants*. Rumors of a possible relationship between the two circulated from several sources during their days on set, and it seems things remain quite friendly despite the professional split. Could they be a new couple in the industry?

Fighting back tears, she picked up the last napkin.

Please know that I consider you the most amazing thing to happen to me in my life, and I thank you for that unconditionally. However, I now fully understand the extent of your commitment to a kind of life I want no part of. I want you to be happy, to achieve all your dreams, but this path to find them is one I cannot and will not travel with you. I have to be true to myself. I have to protect myself. I cannot bear another blow from you, as the last one nearly shattered me. I wish you nothing less than the world, and I know you will have it. I know now you will do anything to get there. But I will always remember you as my baby girl...

With that final goodbye, Jaden fell apart.

She curled into the fetal position and cried herself dry. He had officially written The End on their great romance. Her hopes of sparking a new chance for their love washed away like a grain of sand into an ocean of never mores. She lay there a moment longer, and then wrenched herself to sitting. The voices in her head were angry.

How dare he? He won't even talk to her?
Won't even hear what she has to say?

Maybe he should have, but she created
this situation. She brought this on herself.

Still, he should want to hear
the truth from her.

She had a chance to tell him
six months ago. And she didn't.

Jaden sighed. It wasn't enough to prove her love for him against some asshole from Los Angeles. She was now fighting an assumption—one well-fueled with circumstantial evidence and documentation—as untrue as it might be. She'd lost his trust, and all the privileges that came with it because she'd been chasing what she thought was her dream. And she'd gotten lost along the way.

She wanted to scream because the truth was, she was over it—over the whole thing. Over the bullshit glamour and ridiculous lifestyle she'd been forced to live for this industry. She would trade it all for a different tomorrow, but proving that was something it didn't seem likely she—or anyone else, for that matter—would be able to do. Why couldn't she have woken up with him, talked with him, explained everything? They hadn't exchanged one word the entire night. Had she wasted her chance? At the time she'd felt they'd spoken volumes and the time for conversation would come, but it seemed no real communication had happened at all.

She was lost and alone in a life she'd created. And the one thing she needed, the person who made it all worthwhile, had just put his heart onto a pile of napkins and left her behind.

CHAPTER 21

"Diamonds and Rust"

"This look good?" Liz turned as she put the final touches on the display of colorful boxes and bottles just inside the entrance to Club Essentia. The first shipment of Novella, their new custom product line, had just arrived.

"Perrrrrfect," Ivan purred back to her as he marveled at the display, which held one of his personal dreams, now ready to be unveiled.

"You are talking about the display, right?" She flirted shamelessly and arched her back, he noticed, to emphasize her ass.

"Maybe," he countered as he walked past her toward his office. "What's on the schedule?"

As he entered his office, he glanced out at the view for a moment. It never got old, and despite the turmoil of his final encounter with Jaden, it seemed more brilliant now. *Life* seemed more brilliant now since he'd given himself permission to step out from beneath the rain cloud of doubt and sadness. He'd spent six days now on a clear path forward, on a plan, and the world around him seemed more as it should be: beautiful. He slid behind his desk and started shuffling paperwork, waiting for Liz to follow.

After a moment she strolled in and shut the door behind her. "Your schedule has been crazy this week."

"Tell me about it."

"No, I mean *really* crazy. Thank God it's Friday because I've never seen your bookings this stacked," she said, scrolling through appointments on an iPad. "Doesn't leave much time for…"

"Time for what?" Ivan watched Liz's cheeks pink up.

"You know, a social life."

"You mean a love life?" He smirked, which sent the pink flush into a full-on blush across her face and neck.

Despite her obvious embarrassment, she kept her eyes on him. "You know what they say about all work and no play…"

He laughed and leaned back in his chair with a sigh. "I appreciate the concern, but a full schedule and work is what I need right now."

"All righty then." Liz turned her attention back to her iPad. "You ready?"

"Hit me."

"First you have a ten thirty with Gabriel, and next is an appointment with Mr. Parker. Then I wanted to ask you if I could add a one thirty? Someone's manager called and made an appointment for the VIP sexual health program, so I'm guessing a celebrity of sorts looking for better sex. Ah, aren't we all?"

"Hmmm…" Ivan mused, his interest piqued. "Groovy. What's the name?"

"Ira."

"Never heard of him." He shrugged. "Anything else?"

"Nope. That's it." Liz smiled and left him.

With a few minutes before his patient would arrive, he spun in his seat back to the view. Despite his sunnier outlook, memories of Jaden—her smell, her taste, her touch—flooded his senses whenever he gave himself a moment of down time. Their night together had been physical perfection, but he just couldn't take the accompanying emotional roller coaster. But even though he'd eliminated the Jaden option from his future, he did miss her. And he'd second-guessed his decision to make a clean break more than once. If he were honest with himself, he hadn't stepped fully out from under the dark cloud yet, but he was close. He just needed a bit more time and distraction to get there. And, as he reminded himself often, he was one hundred percent better than he'd been during the darkest days of being guided by the freak and his sexual addictions.

Still, he was grateful when Liz announced Gabriel's arrival, and he had something else to occupy his mind. He transitioned from that appointment directly into his next one, then set to work on his PR blitz for the new line. He worked through a list of patients and media contacts, spreading the word and offering an introduction with a personal touch—his favorite way to do things. His mind wandered in and out of work mode and into dangerous Jaden territory from time to time, but there was nothing to be done. That stupid photo and story in the paper had sealed the deal, shown him what was happening with her in a way he hadn't seen before. And now it wasn't just Micky wanting to talk about Jaden all the time. He could feel people whispering about her, about *them*, everywhere he went.

But there were more calls to be made, and he didn't even notice that he'd worked right through lunch until his computer beeped and the screen indicated that Liz had checked in his next patient. It was one fifteen and the medical assistant was currently sorting this Ira fellow out in the conference room.

He couldn't help but smile as he was sure Liz was probably sitting in on the discussion. The girl loved her celebrities. Ah, to be twenty-five and a cute girl in Miami, he mused.

"Your patient is ready, doctor," Liz chirped over the intercom on his desk. Unable to resist the chance to tease her, he asked, "Is he hot?" in a very effeminate voice.

There was silence for a few seconds, followed by giggling. "No doctor. *He* is not hot."

Hmmm. That's surprising. "Well, bring him on back, girl."

"Yes, sir. I will bring *him* back in two minutes."

Smartass. Ivan jumped up and shrugged on his crisp, embroidered doctor's jacket and pulled his hair into a slick ponytail. He straightened his light blue button up shirt, leaving the top two buttons undone, and brushed his hands over his black slacks.

He returned to his seat and closed out his private email account, which still had several undeleted messages from Jaden. He'd have to deal with that later.

Knock-knock.

"Come on in!" he called, cracking his neck, as his dad told him never to do.

The door swept open, and a book that had been closed for years sprang open to a brand-new chapter. In an instant, Ivan's mind, body, soul, and heart all crashed into each other at the cross streets of What The Fuck and Unfuckingbelievable.

Ira wasn't a man…

The figure seemed to move in slow motion with her eyes trained on his—piercing him, cutting him, stabbing him, just as they'd done so long ago. He was paralyzed and captivated all at once, which was also a familiar feeling. Her eyes were a blue that sparkled like the sea off of a Caribbean island, and they twinkled. He saw himself reflected in their depths, but all he could do was swallow hard and hope he maintained a look of confidence. Inside he was trembling.

Her dark, chestnut brown hair hung in a short bob, skimming along a hard jawline. A low-cut graphic black T-shirt stretched taut across dewy olive skin, and black jeans hung from hips that swung deliciously as "Ira" moved closer and closer.

Her lips parted into the most adorable of smiles, showing just enough teeth to be inviting but not overbearing. She was ever the perfectly coached contestant. Eventually her perfume wafted over, reminding him of all their good times—the moments where life and love ran side by side and nothing else mattered. Roses mixed with hints of lemon…she hadn't changed it.

Ira was indeed not a man. How could he not have not put two and two together? Ira had been a pet name for the girl who'd forced her way into his heart and then broken it, back in the enviable days when work played backup to raw emotion. It had been dumb love—the kind that makes you smile as it rips your heart from your chest. But it had been genuine. He had loved her. Irena Stang.

She had just walked through his door after more than three years, and it seemed she affected him in almost the same way she had when he first laid eyes on her.

Cautiously they came face to face, not saying a thing as they studied each other. Each seemed to wait for the other to make the first move. He looked into her eyes and watched them transition between hundreds of different shades of blue, each more brilliant than the next. And with that, he caved.

"Ira, eh? Well played, girl."

"Well, I thought that if I scheduled using my real name you wouldn't see me." She smiled.

"Actually, I would have said yes and then called in sick."

She burst into laughter, and he joined her, marveling at the peace that washed over him. For a long time he'd imagined this situation over and over—seeing her again—but then its hold on his imagination had subsided. And now that she stood before him, he just felt happy. He was happy with her effort and sneakiness at finding her way to him. As they wrapped their arms around each other, he felt yet another burden released from his body—one he'd suppressed for so long he'd forgotten it, but it had evidently been eating away at him for some time. He squeezed her back and reveled in having come full circle with her. Her presence no longer caused him pain.

When they retreated from their little moment, Ivan noticed Liz out of the corner of his eye. What was she still doing in the room? *Sneaky little thing.* "Um, we're good, Liz. Thank you."

She smiled and pulled the door shut behind her as she went.

"Have a seat." He motioned to the chair in front of his desk and held it for her.

She smiled and sat down. He slid behind his desk, removing his jacket and, with it, all the formalities of doctor-patient relations.

"So…how are you?" she asked. "How've you been? What are you doing? I love this place, Ivan. It's really beautiful."

"Well, you know me," he said, unsure quite where to begin. "Work and play always go hand and hand. This is my baby here, and we're looking to expand this year into a few other markets. But nothing like the *Lifestyles of the Rich and Famous* circles you run in, I'm sure…"

"Oh, stop. It's been quite the ride from reading lines in my one-bedroom apartment, though."

Ivan smiled and nodded.

"I want to know more about this place. All my friends are talking about it, and most of them are patients."

Ivan shook his head and laughed. "Well, it's luxury medicine at its finest. You can never go wrong with offering patients a better quality of life, especially at a premium and via an exclusive membership," he added with a wink.

"And this sexual health—what do you call it? Orgasm augmentation? Where was this when we were together? I mean it was great, but every girl wants more!" She gave him a seductive smile.

Taken aback, he recovered by launching into his standard response. "More powerful and multiple orgasms are easy these days with the right partner and right medication." He smiled and raised his chin. "I can set you up very, very well with the medications. The rest is up to you and your partner."

He sat back in his chair and watched as she lowered her eyes, then looked up through her lashes. "Hmmph, a partner, you say?"

Immediately he recognized her look. It was the one that said naughty, impulsive thoughts were brewing.

Fool me twice... his conscience warned, and he refocused his attention. He needed to find out why she was really here. The more beautiful the rose, the sharper the thorn. And this thorn had cut him once before.

"So what brings you in today? A sexual health assessment? Really?"

"I'm not gonna lie. No—although it is very, very intriguing," she said. "I wanted to see you. I'm starting a shoot here this month, and I'll be here for a while, so I wanted to catch up. I'm scouting with the producers now, and I'll be back in a week to start filming. I just wanted to see if we could go out for a drink or something to talk."

"Hmm..." He paused for a moment, fighting an internal battle. But with his new sunny outlook, why not have a little fun? "Sounds good."

"Okay, well, it's a date then." She stood and prepared herself to leave.

Date? Wow, wow, wow. What? Another traffic jam backed up in his brain. "What?"

"Not a date date, Papi—I mean Dr. Rusilko." She giggled and shrugged. "Sorry, old habit."

The name slammed smack into the ongoing clusterfuck in his muddy mind. He used to live and breathe for his "Goodnight, Papi" and "Good morning, Papi" on their long-distance Skype chats.

"Yes, force of habit."

"Can I text you later this week so we can organize?"

"Yes, of course. Feel free to text anytime." *Slow down!* his defenses screamed.

When she reached the door she stopped and turned to look at him. "Will you answer this time?"

A wave of awkwardness washed over him. He'd ignored many of her messages after their breakup. "Ahhhhh..."

"Ivan, I'm kidding." She turned on the sexy smile. "It was so great seeing you, really. I'm looking forward to our *date*."

"Me too," Ivan said, studying her one more time before she disappeared.

She winked and leaned in for a hug that teetered on the edge of too long.

. "Great," she said, sneaking her tongue through her smile. He couldn't help but watch her ass sway back and forth as she left.

He didn't return to his desk, but instead wandered to the window and felt the epinephrine running through his veins. *What the hell just happened?*

Was he excited? He definitely felt lighter and was happy to say hello after so long, but to take her out? To talk? Did he want to do that? Did she deserve it after what she'd done?

He'd put all of this to rest — this part of life was finished, closed. But now it had been sling-shotted back to the surface, and he was at a loss. But it was a good loss, wasn't it? What harm could come from talking to her? He'd made his decision about her. She couldn't hurt him anymore.

Taking a deep breath, he turned to his desk and realized that position probably applied to another situation as well. He opened the program and finished his email to Jaden. He deleted several sentences that included the words *can't forgive* and *never* and replaced them with:

> Yes, Jaden, I would be happy to talk with you. Tomorrow at 2?
> Let's meet at the point where the boardwalk meets the sand.
> Where the sea turtle watching is best. ;)

He hit send and within minutes received her reply. Folding his arms behind his head, he looked at the ceiling and smiled. *It's a date.*

CHAPTER 22

"Insane"

A soft ocean breeze swelled around the rocks that lined the breakwater at the tip of the boardwalk. Jaden sat alone, just where the sand met the concrete, and watched tourists mill around the beach in front of her. Most wore vibrant man thongs or teeny string bikinis as they absorbed as much fun-in-the-sun as possible. To her left, a bit farther down the beach, a group of teens had picked up a soccer game, using garbage cans as goals and shoes as boundary markers.

With so much activity, this scarcely seemed like the same quiet, moonlit beach that had once played the setting to a magical night of turtle watching. Though it made her a little sad, it was fitting that this would now be the location of the first real conversation she and Ivan had had in six months. She pressed her hands against her hips and smiled when she found the tender bruises that lingered on her body from their night together. That had been communication of some sort, but without a clear message to guide the way forward. What now? Where to begin when they were face to face? She'd arrived an hour early so she could prepare and try to imagine how this talk would go. There must be a way she could make an honest confession *and* convince him to take another chance on her...

She wasn't sure what to think. They'd had an amazing night of mind-bending sex, but then the damned photo of her and Damian had lit a fire of a different kind. He'd agreed to meet, but his email was so innocuous and detached—not terse or mean, but just nothing indicating how receptive he might be. Should she dive right into it all and tell him the whole story right away? Would he listen?

Did it matter? Was she going to try to change his mind? Was it worth it after his very straightforward message? Had he never really trusted her at all? Did she deserve someone who did—or who would at least be willing to listen and talk and try to work things out? Should she try to be just his friend and save what part of their relationship was left? Friendship. With Ivan. Always at her fingertips but never within reach and with no chance in hell he'd ever let her love him again. Unimaginable.

"Heads up!" a voice shouted as a soccer ball came whirling toward her like a black-and-white tornado. Ducking her head she let it whizz past, shooting a surprised look back at the kids.

"Sorry!" the same voice yelled again in a slightly embarrassed tone.

Just then the ball came whizzing back the other way and rolled to a stop in the sand at the players' feet.

"Thanks, mister!" With a final shout and wave, they were back to their game.

"Don't mention it," a voice hollered back, and Jaden froze.

It was still a half hour before he was supposed to be here. Had he come to contemplate the same things she had? A shadowed silhouette formed on the sand in front of her—a shadow with wild hair blowing in the breeze. The presence of someone who, even in shadow, made her heart skip a beat.

She turned and looked up at the man who stood behind her, his features darkened by the sunlight streaming around him. He wore sunglasses, and the wind plastered his white T-shirt to his body.

"Hello, Jaden."

Her mind might have been too foggy to react, but her body took complete control. She shot up from the sand and wrapped her arms around his neck, embracing him as if he might run away. His scent tantalized her, inspiring memories of beautiful moments they'd spent together.

"Hi," she managed to whisper as she released him.

"I see you beat me here."

"Yes, I did, and you're early." She could feel the tears beginning to build.

"You know I'm always early."

"I know, I know." She gave him a shrug and a smile. "Some things never change."

He sighed and turned to gaze out over the water.

She kicked at the sand, took an unsteady breath, and gave him time. When he finally looked back at her, his sunglasses hid whatever was brewing behind his eyes, but her stomach still flipped.

"Want to sit down?" He motioned to the sand.

She took in a deep breath and blew it out. "Okay."

Offering his hand, he helped her sit. He took his place next to her but left enough distance between them to avoid any chance for misinterpretation. They each folded their arms under their knees and looked out into the Atlantic.

"So what's new, babe? How are you?"

His question burned her ego and diluted their history all at once.

"Ivan." Suddenly her strategy was clear. "Don't do that to me. Don't give me some facade like it's all okay. I want you to talk to me without your bullshit, it's-all-okay-because-I'm a-nice-guy act. Something is going on with us. We have a ton to talk about, and I'd like to do that."

He said nothing for a moment. Then sighed. "What?"

"I want you to talk to me like what I did to you mattered. Be pissed at me — be furious with me — but don't be indifferent. I don't want you to diffuse the situation with humor. Be mad for once in your life! But talk to me. I've made mistakes, but I deserve that." The words boiled out from a place in her she didn't know existed.

Removing his sunglasses, he tilted his head and did as she asked. "Okay. Do you want me to tell you I hate who I've become since we broke up? That I've done things to get over you that I never thought I was capable of and I'm disgusted with myself for living that way?"

Jaden opened her mouth to speak, but then closed it again.

"Or how about the fact that no matter how much of myself I devoted to you — no! fuck it! — to us, no matter that I always had the best for you in mind, that wasn't worth any more to you than a goddamn drunken *failed* tryst with a person you claimed to hate.

And yet you couldn't stay away from him! And months later, even after all the shit hit the fan, you couldn't resist the opportunity to promote yourself by taking a flirty, sexy picture with him right here in *my* town where you knew I'd be sure to see it? Being famous is obviously way more important to you than your self respect, or any respect you might have had for me. Which of these options, Jaden?" He paused, glaring at her in a way he had never before. "Which one would you like me to start with? Please pick."

She sat stunned—stunned that he'd taken her up on truly expressing himself, and stunned at the things he had said. Certainly nothing could justify her mistakes and the ways she'd hurt him, but what did he mean she had no self respect? Did he have any idea how hard she'd worked and what a ridiculously high-pressure business television had turned out to be? Didn't he remember how his own career had demanded more and more of his attention just when she needed him most? Perhaps he didn't. Of course he didn't, because he'd refused to talk to her for months! But still, her heart cracked wide open for him. He was so obviously in pain. "Ivan, I—"

He didn't let her finish, just resumed his heartbroken tirade. That seemed to be what he needed. To get it all out. She could do that for him.

"You know, all you had to do was be honest," he spat. "Is that *so* hard? I told you that from the beginning. Honesty is all I need to make a relationship work—even from a distance. I should have learned my lesson the first time, but never in a million years did I think I'd repeat that history with you. The same freaking story—word for word, if you can believe it, which kind of makes me King of the Hopeless, doesn't it?" He shook his head miserably. "Let me guess, you started to wonder…*What's he doing? Is he being faithful? Am I missing out on life?*"

Jaden tried again. "Ivan, yes, I—"

"Don't get me wrong, those are all good arguments, but I thought you were above that," he continued, cutting her off again. "I thought I'd proved at least my loyalty to you. I thought after everything we'd shared—my God, after Napa and our conversation in the vineyard?—that you could come to me. Would it have been that awful, Jaden? Would it be so goddamn scary to say, 'Hey, I'm not feeling so good about this right now, and I need you to tell me I'm a nut job.' Maybe it is my fault, I don't know. But the grass is always going to be greener, you know? I think maybe you're not the kind of person you seemed to be."

Finally seeming spent, he turned away from her to stare into the ocean.

Jaden took a breath and searched for where to begin. "Ivan—"

"I'm not finished," he snapped.

She blinked back at him, tears of sadness and frustration now flowing down her cheeks.

His tone downshifted a notch. "Why couldn't you have been honest with me? Told me what happened? Told me before we had sex in Colorado? And please know that I know you and Damian *didn't* have sex. I know the whole story. I know more than I think even you know."

Her eyes widened. "How?"

"It's never fun listening to another man talk about manipulating someone you love. Especially him." He dropped his head and shook it.

"Ivan, I wanted to tell you. I don't know why I didn't. I was just so scared of losing you. I felt like I was losing myself, and I couldn't bear to risk you too."

"You not telling me is exactly why you lost me. Sure, if you had come to me and told me you made a drunken mistake, I would have been furious. But, I loved you enough that we could have worked through it over time. That would have shown me you were committed to making things right. Shit happens. Trust me, I get it. The fact that you hid it is what breaks me."

The tears increased as the whole horrid mess with Damian washed over her again. They sat silently together until she sighed.

"I mean, God—*Damian* of all people!" he said, rolling his eyes dramatically. "I didn't know you were in to the feminine bad boy type." He poked her in the ribs, eliciting a sad, half-hearted giggle.

"Shut up, you ass," she managed, still struggling to collect herself. She wiped the back of her hand across her cheeks and took a deep breath. "About that night—"

"Stop. I know, Jaden. I know the whole thing. I heard it from the devil's lips himself. I don't need to hear it again. So please don't. I've had enough for one day. You have no idea."

"What do you mean?"

"It isn't important. Look, I get it, though. Trust me. New city, different people, the world at your feet—it can be a crazy situation. I'm guessing thoughts of what I might be doing out here, as well as what you weren't doing there helped fuel the fire that led to everything going up in flames. I swear, word for word, scene for scene, it's the same story I lived with Irena. This is why I was so convinced about not doing the long-distance thing. It's okay at first, but it eats away at your confidence in yourself and the relationship until there's a tipping point. It took me forever to even want to think about who she was again. But surprisingly…"

Ivan paused, almost as if he were trying to figure out what to say or not say. "Surprisingly, here I am, sitting here with you, and so soon after such a disastrous end. I hope you can see how hard this is for me. What I became after you was something I never wanted to be."

"But I'm not her," Jaden said softly, unsure of what his hesitation hinted at. "I know you don't want to relive it, but if you'd just let me talk to you about what happened…You do understand a great deal of it—it's amazing how well you know me—but you don't know everything about me. I can tell you don't because you left the other morning without even a word."

He sighed, and after a moment she felt his hand begin to rub her back. "I wish I felt differently, but I have to protect myself."

"You won't have me," she sobbed while staring at the sand.

"Jaden." He lifted her chin. "I wish like hell I could. You pulled a trigger on my heart, and it has taken everything I have to recover from it. I'm just now getting back to where I was before I met you, and I fear I'll never ever be the man I was with you, and that kills me. But I can't risk you pulling the trigger again. It would end me…I just can't."

She looked up at him through tear-blurred eyes. "This can't be what you want."

"For now, Jaden, it is."

She looked down at the sand again, and in that moment, something shifted inside her. The gaping wound of her need for him began to knit itself together. It would be a magnificent scar, but it was time to give him what he'd asked for—time to heal. "Just please know, I am so sorry. I never imagined any of this happening to us."

"Please don't, Jaden. I know that you're sorry. I'm working through it, as are you."

He took her hand for a moment and gave her a sad smile. The smell of the sea air mixed with his scent and imprinted itself on her senses. She would long remember this day—the day her destiny had changed, whether she believed they belonged together or not.

"So that's it?" she murmured.

"Jaden, nothing is over. It's just changed. What we had was special, and it's ours forever."

He moved his hands to her cheeks and looked into her eyes. "Don't cry because it's over…" He brought his lips to hers ever so softly, and they shared their final taste—the end of a voyage that had taken them from the beaches of Miami to the backwoods of Pennsylvania to the mountains of Colorado.

As their last kiss broke, she finished his sentence. "Smile because it happened."

CHAPTER 23

"Soul to Squeeze"

*J*aden spent the first couple of post-talk days in ugly, oversized clothes, holed up in her apartment, surviving on crappy Chinese takeout and wine. She didn't answer her phone when it rang, but managed to peck out text replies when she wasn't being held hostage by bad reality TV. Sure, she could have changed the channel, but that would have required her to give a shit, and lying brokenhearted and comatose on the couch in a lo-mein haze, she didn't. Then on the third day, she shed the sad clothes, took a shower, and pulled herself together.

Jaden wanted to shop, have a mani and a pedi, and eat something other than cold Chinese noodles. Tasha wanted a rundown on the latest details of her best friend's doomed romantic life: from the alley to the beach. A trip to Lincoln Road was in order.

The girls shopped and chatted as they walked the length of the outdoor mall from Washington Avenue to Alton Road and halfway back again. Jaden was amazed that she actually felt human. It felt good to see the sun.

"I'm hungry. Are you hungry?" Tasha stopped in front of Serendipity 3 and began reading the menu board. "I hear they have a great happy hour."

"And a sundae the size of my head," Jaden said with a laugh. No matter how tempting a chocolate sundae the size of her head might have been, after her cruddy MSG-laced diet of the last few days, she needed real, fresh food. "I'm past that stage of mourning, but thanks."

"Damn," Tasha cursed. "I was willing to blow my diet in your time of need, girl."

Jaden looked over the top of her sunglasses and smiled. "Nice to know your sacrifice has no limits."

"That's the kind of friend I am." Tasha looped her arm through Jaden's and pushed them forward down the mall.

They finally picked a healthier restaurant and snagged an outside table under blue umbrellas that provided the best people-watching views. While they waited for their salads and wine, Tasha launched into a colorful commentary about the passersby. This girls' day out was exactly what Jaden needed to pull herself out of her funk.

About halfway through the meal, her phone rang. 818. The area code had become synonymous with the career she'd thought she wanted and her life's romantic destruction. Without much enthusiasm, Jaden took the call.

"Hello?"

"Jaden, darling, how are you?"

Kevin's voice was almost too much for her. "I'm doing all right. Thank you." She kept her voice pleasant, her answers brief.

"Fabulous. I wanted to call you personally with some great news. They're filming a new movie in Miami starting next week, and I've been contacted to see if you would plan and cook a private dinner for the directors, producers, and stars of the movie at your beloved Bianca."

She opened her mouth to formulate a response, but Kevin forged ahead. What was it with men not letting her talk?

"Of course I said yes!" he continued. "I knew you'd understand the importance of such an event. This could be a huge opportunity for you—a chance to be introduced to some A-listers and maybe garner some connections beyond television, and beyond food, for that matter."

The news and the rush of adrenaline that accompanied it placed a genuine smile on her face for the first time in days. "Wow, Kevin. What a fantastic honor. I'm thrilled!"

"What is it?" Tasha whispered from across the table.

Jaden held up a finger and mouthed *one second.* "Do you have the details?" she asked Kevin. "Who's in the movie? Who's producing it? When do they want to have the dinner?"

The line was silent for an extra few seconds. "I'm not rock solid on all the details yet, but I do know it's an excellent opportunity and one you should really get behind. Lionsgate is the company, and I know a few people there."

"Okay," she said. Quite frankly she didn't know what else to say. "Oh! Does Geoff know? Is Bianca in the loop on this?"

"Yes, they know the dinner will be hosted there and that you've been asked to cook it. I believe Geoff is the contact and is awaiting your response. I also believe you know him rather well?"

Jaden laughed. "Yes, I'd say we know each other rather well."

"Now, listen," he added, his tone turning serious—almost paternal. "I hope you can appreciate what an opportunity it is to be in front of these producers, executives, and directors. The celebrities are really trivial since they're not the ones making decisions. Don't get caught up in the names on the guest list, but fair warning, there's probably some real star power. Just focus on the potential to be the center of attention in a crowd of button pushers."

"Ahhh, okay…" she said, slightly confused. "Is there a name for the movie yet? And you *really* don't know who's involved? Or are you just not telling me?"

"Uh, nope. Not yet. But whoever they are, if you impress them you may have a whole new future in front of you. Lose your focus and I'm afraid you'll be stuck with me for another ten seasons."

"Okay, okay. I get it," she conceded. "Well, let me know the date, and I'm there. I'll get in touch with Geoff shortly."

Jaden looked over to find Tasha about to explode. She suppressed a giggle.

"Excellent," Kevin said. "Oh! And think *seduction* when you plan your menu—sexy foods, aphrodisiacs on steroids, nectar of the gods, that kind of thing. And I think that's all the detail I can give you at this point."

"A seduction menu. Gotcha." Jaden smiled wide and offered Tasha an exaggerated shrug.

"I'll be in touch again soon with more information, and please know this is a great career opportunity—in the kitchen and out. Don't get bogged down in the—"

"Jesus, Kevin! I get it. I will. I'm all business," she assured him.

"Okay, thank you," he replied. "I'll call you soon."

"Bye."

Jaden clicked her phone off and looked at Tasha, puzzled.

"Oh, you better start talking *now!*" Tasha announced, looking like she might leap across the table.

"Well, apparently some bigwigs want me to cook a private dinner for the cast and crew of a movie that starts shooting here next week." She watched Tasha's face light up. "The best part is the dinner's at Bianca!"

The girls squealed in unison, earning them dirty looks from the adjacent tables.

"Who's gonna be there? What celebs?"

"Well, he didn't say. He was all about the fact that it was a networking possibility for me with the directors and execs, but he danced around the other details. I don't care, really. It's exciting!"

"You aren't even a little bit curious?"

"Well, of course I am, but I have to cook regardless. So that's going to be my focus."

"So serious!" Tasha rolled her eyes. "Can't we squeal again?"

Jaden indulged her with a particularly over-the-top shriek, and their squeals turned to giggles just as their overpriced salads arrived.

"Well, I'm sure you will rock star them, girl. See? Now don't you feel better?" Tasha speared some chicken and lettuce and gestured with her fork. "I told you. You get *your* shit together, get your mojo all shined up, and this clusterfuck with Ivan is going to just fall away. Where better to get your confidence back than in the kitchen *at Bianca?* That place is your home turf."

"You're right," she conceded, though she reflected for a moment on the state of her and Ivan's non-union. "But I just miss him. I can't help that. We've texted back and forth a bit for the past couple days, but it's such a diluted, stiff exchange." Jaden waved her hands uselessly.

"Is he being mean?" Tasha asked. "Because you can't—"

"No, he's pleasant enough, but there's no personality, no affection, no depth. I don't think he's ever going to have a conversation of substance with me again. He's walled himself off. It just seems like the precursor to a dying friendship, and since the rest of the relationship is already gone, I don't see the point of delaying the inevitable. Perhaps a clean separation is better…"

"Well, I know that sucks, but you might be right. If he's not open to putting things back together, you can't repair it on your own." Tasha was quiet for a moment, then smiled brightly. "You'll just have to focus on kicking ass!"

"I know you're right." Jaden sighed. "It's just going to take some time. Right now I really miss the sweet nothings he used to send me."

She held her wrist up to examine the fading yellow of one of the last remaining marks on her body, a bittersweet memento from her night with Ivan. She'd cataloged all these little marks on her body since then and cherished them. This small, barely there yellow thumbprint on her wrist and one small spot on her left hip were all that remained. When Ivan's mark on her body was gone, she'd have nothing left of him. *He'd* be gone. Her skin would be healed but her heart would be scarred forever.

"But he has let me go," she continued after a moment. "I promised myself I'd try until he told me no, and the other day at the beach, he did. Sooo…The worst part is I know he still loves me, loves what we had together, but he's too afraid to move forward. He'd rather have nothing than be hurt again, and I hate that—I hate that I caused it." She shuffled the mixture of greens, cheese, nuts, and salmon around on her plate with her fork. "But there's nothing I can do. He won't let me."

Tasha patted her hand, but remained silent.

"I'm just tired of feeling so lonely," Jaden added. "I'm tired of waking up to utter despair. So it's time to move forward, and let's start with this kick-ass movie dinner, right?"

"Now you're talking!" Tasha practically cheered. "Look out for this bitch!"

Jaden laughed and felt a teensy bit better. Who knows, maybe sometime soon she might catch a glimpse of the girl she'd been before insecurity took her out at the knees.

CHAPTER 24

"Father and Son"

"Matthew, what is this?"

Ivan turned to find his mother holding up the box of condoms he kept in his bathroom. And she'd used his first name, so he knew he needed to think fast. They'd sprung this trip on him rather suddenly and refused to take no for an answer, so he hadn't had time for as much "tidying" around his apartment as he might normally do.

"Mom, what do I specialize in? Sexual health. What do I promote? Sexual health. So what do you think I provide to my patients? Sexual health products." He gestured toward the box with a flourish. "I just happen to have some at home."

She raised a skeptical eyebrow.

"Aw, crap!" his father cut in. "You found my stash. I was hoping to surprise you later."

She gasped and rolled her eyes at her husband. "Don't you start getting goofy on me now. You get like this every time we go on vacation."

"Yes, but it has worked for the past thirty-eight years, so something about it must be right." His dad chuckled, but Ivan caught his *you owe me* look clear as day.

"Sometimes I wonder," she muttered as she turned back toward the bathroom with the white box.

His dad disappeared into the kitchen while Ivan schlepped the rest of their bags to the guest room.

"So how are you?" his mother asked as she followed him down the hallway.

"Good! Business couldn't be better. We're already looking to expand to Monaco or Casa de Campo at the end of the year maybe and then—"

"No, I mean how are *you?* Personally."

Her voice softened, and her meaning was apparent. How was he since he and Jaden broke up? He had no idea how to answer.

Though he felt terrible about it, he'd avoided all talk of Jaden with his parents since it happened. Maybe he was embarrassed by how it ended, or maybe talking through it with them would make it all too real. Keeping it to himself allowed him to cling to the hope that perhaps someday they'd reunite. If he exposed even the slightest hint of her failed infidelity, it might change his family's view of her. Above all, he was so thankful he hadn't shared his plans to ask her to marry him. Explaining that night to his family would have brought him to his knees.

It had been bad enough as it was. Ivan still remembered the day he'd told his mother Jaden was not a part of his life any more. Her silence and broken voice over the phone had conveyed her sorrow perfectly. He knew she'd loved Jaden as her own, even after just a short time. When she asked what happened, the only response he could offer that wouldn't break her heart was, "we just couldn't make it work."

He put down the bags and arranged them at the foot of the bed. "Mom, I'm good."

She crossed her arms and looked at him with kind eyes. "Really?"

Ivan leaned against the door jamb, crossed his arms, and crossed one foot over the other. "Really. Work keeps me focused on the future. There's all sorts of potential. Yesterdays are to be looked at over your shoulder. If you keep them in front of your face you may miss what the future holds. A smart lady once told me that," he said with a wink.

"Work is great, but someone once told me money is worthless when compared to life's pricelessness."

He shoved his hands in his pockets and leaned forward at the waist. "Yes, and the man who said that is telling you he is okay now."

"Well, I just can't help feeling you haven't been yourself," she said, still evidently not satisfied. "The last few months you scared me and your—"

Pop! The sound of a sparkling Shiraz being uncorked echoed into the bedroom. Ivan looked over his shoulder around the door frame and then back to his mother. They shared a smile.

"Well, Dad's found the wine…" Ivan offered. "Shall we?"

His mother stepped toward him, but the smile slipped from her face, and a mother's worry returned to her expression. "I just don't understand what could have happened."

He sighed. How could he reassure her? "You know, I wasn't okay for a while there. You're right. And I'm sorry. I know I shut you out. I wasn't myself. I hated who I was and how I felt. But I am much better now — not perfect, but better. So please, let's not dwell on this. I want you guys to have some fun while you're here. It's been too long since you've been down."

"Nobody needs to be perfect," she said as she hugged him like only she could.

"Thank you guys for being there even when I wasn't. Thank you for worrying. But please stop now!" He squeezed her small frame and nuzzled the top of her head with his cheek as they walked back down the hall.

"Are these for me?" his father asked as soon as they reappeared in the front room. One hand held an open bottle of wine with three glasses hanging from his fingers and the other held a full bag of fresh cigars.

"You waste no time, do you?" Ivan released his mother and reached for the wine bottle and glasses. "Yes, they're for you."

"Nice. Now, what'd I miss?" He looked from Ivan to his wife and back.

"Nada," Ivan said, giving his head a definitive shake. "Let's get this poured and you toked up." He put his arms around his parents' shoulders and led them to the balcony.

"Ahhh!" his father said approvingly as they stepped outside. "The view's been upgraded. And it wasn't bad before!"

Tipping the bottle toward the three glasses, Ivan chuckled as they explored the balcony, studying all the different angles. He passed each of them a glass and offered a toast: "To family, the nonfiction aspect of a fictitious world."

"Salud!"

They clinked their glasses together with a smile, and Ivan almost felt comfortable in their presence. But he could still feel his mother's lingering gaze.

"So what do you want to do while you guys are here?"

"Just relax and talk. It's been forever, so we're happy just to see you." His mother offered her usual response. Ivan smiled, but felt the slightest touch of dread.

"Well, sure, we can talk," his dad said. "But I also want to go down there and get some sun."

Ivan laughed when he identified where his father was pointing. The pool deck below was dotted with lounge chairs, which were inhabited by what could easily be the Victoria's Secret Angels.

"John!" his mother scolded.

"Is it like that every day?"

"Give or take."

"Also, let's look for a condo in this building," he added, waggling his eyebrows at his wife.

"I'm happy you're here. I've missed you both," Ivan said. He smiled, but his father was too busy fumbling with wineglass in one hand a lighter and cigar in the other. He grabbed the lighter and sparked a flame for him. "Well, maybe one of you more than the other."

"Smart ass." His dad punctuated his opinion with a cloud of sweet-smelling smoke.

"You guys hungry?"

"Starving," Marie responded, finishing her wine in one gulp.

"Okay, let's go grab a bite."

"Not me," his father replied. "I can eat in Pennsylvania. I'm getting some sun."

Ivan joined his mother in eyeing him suspiciously.

"On the beach, okay?!"

"Riiiiiiiiiight." Ivan shook his head as he too finished his wine and led his mother back inside. "But don't wear a thong or anything that might embarrass me too much."

"Shh! Don't give him any ideas," his mother warned.

She disappeared into the guest bedroom to get ready while Ivan searched for a towel for his father. He chose the most colorful, flashy one he could find and couldn't help but snicker as he handed it to him.

"Really? Do I get a purse with this?"

Ivan laughed and turned toward his bedroom, but he was stopped by a hand on his shoulder. When he faced his father, all traces of joking had left his face. "You okay, son?"

Both of them? How am I going to do this? Ivan wondered. But then he reminded himself how lucky he was that they cared so much. *Thank God for such a beautiful family.*

"Yeah, I am, big guy. Thank you."

His father nodded, swirled the towel around his shoulders, and wrapped Ivan in a dual Rusilko bear hug, for which neither person had the upper hand.

Ivan took his mother to eat at a local spot with a great little patio. It was no Lincoln Road, but the food was good, and it was a nice day to eat outside. Miami Beach people watching might have been a bit much for his poor mother anyway.

"So tell me about Meadville," he said after their food had arrived. "Anything new?"

"It's pretty much the same way you left it."

"And PJ and Elise?"

"They're just curious as to what's happened to their brother for the last little bit."

Dropping his fork, he looked at his plate for a moment before facing his mother. She was not giving up on this. It was his habit, albeit a bad one, to go off the grid when he was overwhelmed. When it was because of his schedule or work, he was pretty good about calling and checking in, but this mess with Jaden had him really checked out. He'd managed his friends easily enough—a laugh and a quick conversation could shake most of them off. Except for damned Micky. But his mother was a different story.

"Mom, really, now I'm okay. I was a bit twisted for a while after Jaden and I split—well, a long while to be honest, but I got through it. Not the way I wanted to, but I did."

"Got through, or are getting through?" She looked at him with a furrowed brow.

"Getting. But almost there."

Why was she so insistent about this? She usually gave him his space once it was apparent he didn't want to discuss something.

"Well, I just remember how you were after Irena, and we really thought Jaden…Well, we've just been worried. We don't like seeing our son like that."

Ah. Now he understood the concern and the "random" request to come visit. This wasn't the first surprise trip John and Marie had made to Miami Beach, and it probably wouldn't be the last. If he'd just pulled it together enough to call or to answer their calls, he wouldn't now have to submit to his mother's in-person questions and more than that, he wouldn't have to see the worry and concern on her face now. His father had likely snuck his way over to the pool beauties by now, but his mother truly needed some reassurance that he was okay.

"Mom, please be assured that I am on the upswing. I love that you two came down, and it means the world to me, but you don't have to be concerned." He smiled at her across the table, praying his words and his eyes conveyed sincerity and confidence to ease her mind.

"Okay, well, know that we love you, and you can count on us for anything."

"I do. Believe me, I do."

"So do you see Jaden anymore? Or talk to her? She just was a great girl…"

Unsure how to proceed, he shoveled in a bite of fish and took a sip of wine to give himself time to think. He made a great display of chewing. "Yeah, I saw her just the other day, and I think we're okay. She's doing very well with her career, and I'm happy for her. We're moving forward as friends."

As he spoke he was a bit surprised to realize he did want to be her friend. Despite the pain, he missed her presence in his life.

His mother smiled back at him and finally started to work on her chicken Marsala.

"I saw Irena the other day too," he added and watched her stop eating mid-bite. He stuffed in another mouthful to buy some time.

"And…" his mother pressed.

And what? he thought to himself. *Why the hell did I bring that up?*

"Ah, she's doing well, as I'm sure you know from all the magazines. She's about to start a new movie."

"And?"

"And what?"

"Where did you see her? What happened that led you to see her?"

"Nothing. Just coincidence, I suppose. She was scouting locations. It was nice though."

His mother was quiet another moment, as if waiting to see if he would say more, but when he didn't she finally sighed and spoke. "Okay, well, please tell both of them we all say hello, and we wish them the world."

"Will do, boss." He smiled, hoping this topic had been closed.

Then his mother smiled at him a bit strangely. "You know, sometimes no matter how much you think you're giving or doing to make a relationship work, unless you're speaking the same language, it doesn't matter." She narrowed her eyes. "And I'm not talking English here, kid."

Despite his desire to be done with this conversation, Ivan was now intrigued. "Then what are you talking about?"

"Maybe Irena never heard 'I love you' when you said it to her," his mother said. "Maybe she only heard it when you gave her something pretty or showered her with gifts?"

"You think?" Ivan asked, just before he took a long, thoughtful draw on his wine.

"And maybe Jaden only heard it when you spent time with her?"

"Are you going all psychoanalyst on me now?"

"I think maybe someone should, don't you?" she said with a laugh.

"Ha, ha. Very funny." He lobbed a carefree wink and a smile across the table at her, but his mind churned around her words. *Ugh.* Why was she stirring all this up again? "Excuse me for a second. I need to hit the head."

He stood and made his way to the restroom, his head swimming a bit. His mother's insights were good—a little too good, if he was being honest—but he'd already walked through the fire. He was on the other side of the pain where Jaden was concerned now, and rehashing it wasn't going to make it better. Telling his mother all the nasty details wasn't going to make *her* feel better either. He decided that if he had any hope of surviving the weekend, he was going to have to keep them entertained and avoid any more of these conversations.

Of course that would mean he'd have to take some time away from the spa, but if he couldn't take time out for his family and to enjoy life a little, what was he working so hard for?

He snagged the phone from his pocket to check for anything pressing since he'd silenced it at the beginning of lunch. No business, amazingly, but a text from AVOID:

> Hi, Ivan. I see your parents are in town.
> Please give them my best.

And a text from Irena, who was still labeled Mami:

> Hi Papi. Tell John and Marie hello and that I miss them
> very much. Looking forward to seeing you soon. ;)

"How the hell?" Ivan wondered aloud. It was as if two ghosts had been sitting at the table with him. Then he realized. *Facebook. Gets me every time.* The sound of splashing on the floor alerted him that his concentration had wandered too far. "Fuck." He tucked his phone away and finished with the necessary business of taking a proper piss.

Nevertheless, he remained a bit in awe that both the loves he'd had in his life were in the same town, on same message stream, and of the same mind-set. It also seemed strange that his phone setting for Jaden was tied to the dark time when he hadn't wanted to hear from her, yet Irena's was still his affectionate name for her, which conjured up their happiest times. Perhaps both contact settings needed a change, but he couldn't bring himself to do anything with either of them. His mind was completely scrambled as he zipped up and washed his hands. He looked into the mirror and shook his head at who he saw. *Ay, ay, ay.*

CHAPTER 25

"Drive"

*I*t turned out that the first few weeks Jaden had in Miami — the ones where she couldn't quite get herself into vacation mode yet — were the only vacation she was really going to get. After Kevin got things rolling with the event she hosted, she'd been nearly non-stop on the wine and food events circuit. Three — no, four — in the last month had slammed her back into the tilted, celebrity version of reality. She got to cook a little and do some fan events, but the press junkets — with their endless talking about nothing and constant dodging of questions about her personal life — left her drained. Was this really the career and "success" she'd worked so hard to achieve?

She'd been almost completely at a loss when she reached out to Geoff. Thank God for him. They'd scheduled a meeting to plan the movie dinner, but Jaden soon found herself at Bianca in most of her spare moments. She met with staff in and out of the kitchen to prep for the event, but she also just observed. Watching Geoff manage the restaurant with such passion and precision inspired her. She'd forgotten what it was like to be part of a small, well-trained, professional environment where everybody has your back and everybody has pride in the "family." Her time back there, back in a more natural orbit, made it easier for her to filter the now and focus on the future. She'd come to love networking with the non-celebrity chefs on the food and wine events circuit, and she was beginning to see where she might want to end up once again.

However, at the moment, her now and her future had ganged up on her in a furious assault of nerves. She'd been running around her apartment in various stages of dressed and undressed for the last half hour, but now she stood in nothing but her panties staring into her closet. An anxious rush blazed up from her stomach — a physical manifestation of her impending, highly publicized return to Bianca. Her brain was busy processing and reviewing the complicated Menu of Seduction she'd created, which kept her from being able to focus properly on what to wear…

If anyone thought *One Hot Kitchen* maven Jaden Thorne had lost her creative edge when she went Hollywood, they were sorely mistaken. She could still carve out one hot, sexy menu. Appetizers would include lobster, avocado, and mango salad, tomato basil soup, burrata bruschetta with grilled figs, and chargrilled oysters with Roquefort cheese and red-wine vinaigrette. For the entrée, guests would have a choice of honey-roasted hens with pomegranates, grilled tuna (of course), or grilled asparagus with lemon and honey-ginger carrots. And for dessert, nutmeg donuts, strawberry-rhubarb ice cream with honey-hazelnut biscotti, and dark chocolate chili truffles. She'd approved a signature pomegranate martini and left it to the sommelier to sort out the wine pairings. It was a feast of sex on a plate, in a bowl, or swimming in a crystal glass for a full five courses. If these diners didn't get lucky tonight, well, that just wasn't her fault.

She'd felt a little bad when she sprang the sexy, aphrodisiac-specific menu on her one-night-only extra sous chefs and line cooks, but she knew Bianca's executive staff well enough to be sure they could handle it. She gave them her best pep talk to help them rise to the challenge. This was her night. If she pulled this off, she'd prove she was still a rock star in the kitchen, not just on TV.

Jaden carried a dress over to the mirror for consideration. She smiled and then growled fiercely at her reflection before dissolving into giggles. Despite the relentless intrusion of her L.A. life, her time in Miami Beach had energized her. She knew in her heart she still loved Ivan, but because of that love, she was willing to let him go, as he wanted her to. At least most of the time she was. The odd flare of frustration or sadness could overtake her at any moment, but she was getting better and better at working through them. Her only path was forward, and the wound on her heart would heal in time.

However, what her time away had not managed to do was cultivate much enthusiasm for her return to *One Hot Kitchen*. She couldn't decide whether the whole experience was tainted for her now, or if it had never been what she dreamed it would be in the first place. Either way, she was a little sad that her time here was coming to an end. Tasha and Micky had taken a trip to the Keys, so she'd already told them goodbye, and after this final hurrah at Bianca, it was time to go back to her commitments in L.A. *One Hot Kitchen* had to be her priority, but after that and in every spare second she could carve out, she was going to build a new life she could enjoy and be proud of.

"Shit!" she gasped out loud as she realized her go-to Miami Beach stylist was now in Key West. She agonized for a moment, but then laughed at herself. A simple ponytail would totally work because after all, she was going to be sweating her ass off in the kitchen. There was *real* work on the docket tonight.

She returned to her closet for more staring. She sifted past a pink dress, a yellow skirt, a black business suit, and more colorful, flowy gowns than one girl should own. None of them seemed quite right. She needed to turn a head or two, but not look like she was trying too hard…and then there was the chef's jacket she'd have on over it for most of the evening. *Ugh.* But then she saw it: a girl's best friend. Not diamonds, but the little black dress. Put on a pair of pumps and she was ready.

She pulled out the dress and returned to the mirror for a final check. *Ivan loved short dresses,* her brain announced, and images of what had happened when she wore such dresses in Miami Beach bubbled up in her thoughts. She closed her eyes for a moment, and with a sigh and a shake of her head refocused her thoughts. Not now. Not tonight. Move forward. Yes, this dress would be perfect. She could rock high heels, get her legs out there, and still maintain professionalism with the white jacket on top.

She slipped into the slim little dress and collapsed on the bed. Exhaling she watched the fan turn lazy circles against the ceiling for a moment. Her mind turned similar circles as she wondered for the zillionth time who would be attending her dinner. She was hours away from yet another major transition and life decision, and she did everything she could to temper the excitement and anxiety. Potential investors? Maybe. A possible partner? Maybe. New loyal palates who would frequent the restaurant she dreamed about opening? Maybe. She laughed at the absurdity of it all. Investors? Partners? A new business? She sounded just like Ivan. *Ivan…*

Breathing in and out, in and out, she found her center and rose for the next challenge. She headed for the bathroom, snagged her makeup and brush, and went to work. "Why the hell did I tell them I didn't need a glam squad for this?" she wondered aloud.

She ran the brush through her long, black hair and pulled it into a low ponytail at the nape of her neck, leaving a few strands loose around her face. She brushed on a neutral but shimmery eye shadow, but then drew a dark, dramatic liner along the top of her lashes, followed by mascara, paying special attention to the outer lashes. She finished with a soft blush on the apples of her cheeks, a swipe of color on her lips, and some pineapple gloss.

"Thank you, Kat," she said as she nodded in approval at her reflection. She hadn't been just napping or gossiping during all those hours in hair and makeup. She'd actually learned some tricks! She was a lot more capable than she knew. It was time she remembered that.

She packed up her makeup bag and the rest of the little beauty bottles she always accumulated when she traveled, then carried them over to where her bags stood open. Her packing was already underway.

She took a final look in the mirror and felt satisfied. She then sifted through her jewelry, and her eyes and heart came to rest on a turtle bracelet. An inconvenient flashback to their room at Chateau Marmont floated across her memory, but she managed to smile. She slipped on the bracelet, enjoying the weight of it and the cool metal against her skin. *Why not?* Jaden pulled out her black patent high heel Louboutins, slipped them on, and turned off the lights. She gathered a garment bag with her chef's jacket and a bag of her hard core kitchen gear just inside the front door, and after one last check in the mirror, set out for the night.

The menu still dominated her thoughts, but as she rode the elevator down she began to feel another rush of excitement about the guest list. She smiled at her much-improved confidence and schmoozing ability—something else that would always remind her of Ivan. He'd taught her so much when she was new on this scene. Maybe she could do this friend thing with him. After all, they'd had so many stupid, fun times together, and he was a valuable resource and advisor. Maybe things could eventually be mostly the same, just minus the sex. *Oy, the sex.* God, what she wouldn't give for one more doctor's appointment and a little green pill. But they'd been more than that, so it could work, right?

As the elevator opened she decided to treat herself to a cab. She didn't need any extra distractions tonight. Outside, the breeze carried a whisper of jasmine, just as it had that night in Sarasota, and a shiver passed through her. Perhaps tonight might be another she would remember forever. Her yellow chariot pulled up, and she opened the door, pausing to revel in the possibilities ahead before she slid into the backseat.

"Bianca, please."

CHAPTER 26

"Bad Moon Rising"

After a long but fun and surprisingly relaxing (despite its intense beginning) weekend with his parents, Ivan had delivered them to the airport with plenty of time to check their bags and make it to the gate. His mother was busy looking for their itinerary when his father pulled him away from the car parked at the curb. With Dad, you never knew if it was going to be a corny, dirty joke or a pearl of real wisdom, and either way, you didn't want to miss it. Ivan leaned in toward his father and waited.

"Ivan, the only advice I can give you about love is this: When you find that one little thing about someone you can't find in anyone else—no matter how small it is—that thing that completely shuts down whatever else you're doing? She's the one. Find that, and you've found her. That one little thing for me was your mother's laugh. Okay?" Then he'd grabbed him in a hug so tight, he could still feel his arms across his back. "Think about that."

Still eyeing him, his father had stepped back, and Ivan scarcely remembered what his mother had said as she hugged him goodbye. Hours later his father's words continued to bounce around the back of his mind, and he still couldn't say for sure whether he'd ever experienced that with anyone before.

"Ass," he mumbled to himself, smiling and shaking his head. His dad had an uncanny ability to stir things up and make him think.

Defining that one little thing was probably easy in hindsight, after you'd found her. But back to the task at hand, he told himself.

"What to wear to dinner with a girl who broke your heart…" He stood, naked and stumped, inside his closet, finding no inspiration among the pants on the left or the shirts and sport coats on the right. He ran his hands over their fabrics, guessing and then second-guessing himself.

"She said casual dinner and low key…" So he settled on a pair of dark blue Triachy jeans, sent to him by the designer, and a white button-down shirt. Then he hesitated, remembering that her definition of low key usually involved a red carpet. He grabbed a brown sport coat just to be safe. Exhausted by the process, he tossed his selections on the bed and trotted out to grab a bottle of water. He surveyed his apartment as he passed and was proud of the job he'd done cleaning up the place. Okay, proud of the adjustments he'd made after the housekeeper had done the heavy work.

Why was it that cleaning could be both a pain in the ass and a joy, depending on the situation? The times he'd cleaned Irena's apartment while she was at work were some of his happiest memories of their time together. His tidying always ended with her coming home, dropping her bad mood, smiling her smile, and squealing "Papi" as she ran to him and jumped into his arms. Now he'd relegated cleaning to a lovely woman he paid to come once a week because he didn't have the time or inclination to do it for himself. "Relativity," he quipped, offering his water bottle in toast to the air around him.

The real question was why he was so intent on having a clean apartment in the first place. Was he planning on bringing someone home tonight? The thought paralyzed him for a second, but he kept moving. It had been just long enough for him to realize the magnitude of what a clean apartment meant, but not long enough to contemplate whether he meant to use it.

Back in his room, he pulled on his briefs and pants and checked his phone.

See you at 830, Papi.

A shiver ran down his spine, but he could not discern whether it was good or bad. Papi? She'd jumped right back into his pet name so soon? Interesting. Sure, she was Mami on his phone contact list, but he wasn't *calling* her that. Still, they'd had some wonderful times together. What if she did want to come back? Was that a line he'd be willing to cross?

No. Don't get carried away, man, he told himself. This is just a friendly bite to eat—innocent and platonic, right? Friends eat dinner together all the time. That's what they agreed on. The "date" label she threw in at the end was a joke, right? Yes, it had to have been. *Fuck it!* his mind screamed, silencing the mental jerk-off session. He'd cleaned his apartment, for Christ's sake. *Fuck it. It's a date, and that's it.* He threw his shirt on and buttoned it up. *Let's see where tonight takes us.*

He rummaged through the drawer for a pair of cufflinks and pondered a variety of options: turquoise, tiger's eye, or sea turtles. The first two were a toss-up, but for some reason the third pair called to him. They'd been a surprise gift from Jaden on one of her weekends in Miami. Now, looking down at them in the drawer, Ivan wished for a moment this "date" was with her. *Ugh.* He shook the feeling off. *Stand your ground!* He had to stick to the commitment he'd made himself. They were just cuff links, and besides that, they were more casual than the other pairs. Jesus Christ, was he really this indecisive about a fucking pair of cuff links? No. Not anymore. Sea turtles would do just fine.

He spritzed on cologne, tucked his brown jacket over his arm and was ready for his dinner/meeting/date with Irena. He couldn't help but remember the first time he'd known she would hold a special place in his heart. On an impromptu trip to Chicago they'd enjoyed everything the windy city had to offer. The aquarium, stadiums, and pizzas deeper than he'd thought possible were experienced together under a veil of romance. They'd shared countless glasses of wine and so many stories. At the end of one day he'd laid back on the hotel room bed and listened to her talk, her thick accent growing stronger and more pronounced with each drink.

The minute she'd dropped her head, keeping her eyes fixed on him with the sexiest of smiles, his heart had burst forth to profess his love verbally. The three little words rang through a wintery night as she professed hers as well. Then they'd devoured every inch of each other's bodies. It was a magical night. In hindsight, when it all fell apart, there hadn't been much of a foundation for the fairy tale they built, but that didn't make it any easier when he was standing alone in the rubble. The thought of rebuilding all that was tempting and threatening at the same time.

"Ay," he muttered as he surveyed the room one last time and patted his pockets for keys, phone, and credit cards. He adjusted his collar and headed out into an uncertain night with even more uncertain potential.

CHAPTER 27

"Won't Back Down"

The kitchen crew and wait staff scattered like confetti when Jaden wrapped up the pre-event meeting, and she smiled at the hum of activity around her as the kitchen came to life. But after a moment her smile faltered a bit. The final details she'd been missing about this dinner had fallen into place, but they now hung around her neck like a lead weight.

You can do this, she told herself. If Irena Stang had orchestrated this whole night in an attempt to embarrass her or put her on notice, she was going to be disappointed. This was *her* house, and if she could just focus on the food and flavors, then no one—not even the infamous Irena Stang—could shake her.

As she deliberated about whether or not she had time to call Tasha to commiserate, her phone buzzed in her pocket. She grabbed it, and once she saw who it was, headed straight through the galley and into the sub-zero.

"Hello, Kevin. What can I do for you?"

"Ahh, hello, Jaden. Just wanted to check in and see if you were all ready for the big night."

"Just finished a meeting with the staff, and now I need to hop to it. But since you called, Kevin, why didn't you tell me that this whole dinner was for Irena Stang?"

"Because it's not, Jaden."

She sighed impatiently. "But you knew she'd be here, and you knew she was—"

"Whoa. I'm going to stop you right there," Kevin replied. "Who's around that table is irrelevant. You just have to wow them. Doesn't matter who they are."

Jaden paced the freezer. "Irena Stang at my table makes a difference, Kevin. Don't you think a heads up might have been nice?"

"Frankly, I wasn't sure that would do you any good at all," he said.

"Whatever. Fine. I just have one other question. When you first told me about this dinner, you said someone had specifically requested that I cook."

"Yes, that's true."

"So who asked for me? Was it production or someone else?"

Kevin didn't reply.

"Tell me."

"Production asked on behalf of..."

She stopped pacing. "Irena Stang."

"I didn't say that."

"You didn't have to," she said as she shoved open the fridge and returned to the bustling kitchen.

"No matter what, this is an amazing professional opportunity, Jaden. For you and for the show. Please make the most of it."

"I'm not stupid. And I have to go. I have a kick-ass dinner to prepare."

"Thatta girl," Kevin replied.

"Sure thing."

"Oh, one more thing," he added.

"What's that?" she asked, now tapping her foot and itching to get started.

"I hear you're coming back to L.A. tomorrow."

"Yep."

"I'm glad to hear it," he said with a smile in his voice.

She laughed as she shook her head. "You didn't think I would, did you?"

"To be honest? I wasn't so sure."

"It's nice to know you have such faith in me, Kevin."

"It's not about faith. I just know things can change, and I also know this last season wasn't easy for you. I really do understand that." He paused for a moment. "I'm not gonna lie and say I didn't have a plan B."

"Always have a plan B, huh, Kev?"

"In this business, you'd be a fool not to."

"Gotta do what you gotta do, I suppose."

"Yep. But I'll see you when you get back."

"Yes, sir!"

"Knock 'em dead, kiddo."

"Thanks." Jaden zipped over to the break room where she threw her phone in her handbag, kicked off her high heels, slipped into kitchen clogs, and shrugged on her jacket. "Plan B, my ass," she muttered as she dressed. *Plan B.* If Kevin had a plan B, shouldn't she have a plan B too? And what if plan B looked better to both of them than plan A? Jaden sighed and smoothed her jacket. At the moment her only plan was to go out there and cook her ass off. She swung the door open and nearly crashed into Geoff.

"There you are!" he said. "Listen, I wanted to tell you — he made me promise not to give you all the details." He looked down a bit sheepishly.

"It's fine, Geoff," she said. "I can handle it."

"I never had any doubts."

Jaden gave him a quick hug. "Thank you. Truly."

"Come on now," he urged with a smile. "We've got everything ready to go. We just need someone to start barking orders and bossing everyone around."

"That I can do!" she said with a laugh. She followed him into the work space and made her first stop checking on the sous chefs. Then, free of an executive chef's usual long-term management duties, she picked up her knives and joined in the chopping, mincing, and dicing of fresh ingredients. It wasn't long before all thoughts of Irena — or anything else — were banished, and she was lost in her art and her work. By the time the first hors d'oeuvres were prepped and plated for passing, she'd found her groove.

CHAPTER 28

"Don't Let Me Be Misunderstood"

Ivan maneuvered Candy through side streets and back alleys, avoiding the rush on Miami Beach as he picked his way across the island to pick up Irena.

"Well, let's see how late she's going to be." He messaged her during one of his many stops along the way.

> There in 5. Are you on your usual schedule?

Her time-management skills had always been an issue for them. But immediately his phone rumbled with a response.

> Smartass! I'm ready.
> Message me when you're here and I'll come out.
> Go to side street entrance.

Surprised, he smiled as he typed a quick response.

> Apparently being a big shot makes one punctual.

Was he being too flirty or just friendly, he wondered *after* he hit send. When his phone buzzed again, he saw a smiley face giving him the finger. He laughed and almost skimmed a parked car.

As he turned down the side street that led to the Setai, an influx of nerves bombarded him, and he realized that, apart from the brief whatever-that-was in his office the other day, he hadn't spoken to her, let alone seen her, since the proverbial elevator doors closed on their relationship three years ago. The twenty minutes in his office were powerful and intriguing, but not nearly enough time to prepare for an actual evening together where conversation was required and the visual contact might be more than he could bear.

He slowed to a stop, looking down the alley where he was to pick her up. If he turned around now, he could be back to his place in fifteen minutes, bottle of wine open in twenty, and a good buzz going in forty-five—the easy way out. Or he could pick her up and pull a night like he'd had with Jaden a few weeks ago—the evil and fun way out. Or he could man up and take an old girlfriend out to a casual dinner—just to catch up and maybe steal a bit of closure along the way.

Man up it is.

He typed out a text.

Outside.

"Let's rock," he mumbled as he put the car back in drive.

He rounded the corner and stopped just short of the entrance, where he put Candy in park and began to play the waiting game. His phone buzzed again. He half expected to see a message asking for fifteen minutes, but instead it was a note from AVOID:

I hope you have a great night, Ivan. xoxo

He froze as if he'd been caught, and the heat of adrenaline flared through his chest. But he wasn't breaking any rules—well, maybe his own—but nevertheless, a small sliver of guilt wormed its way through him as he composed a response.

I hope u have a better one, Jaden. xoxo

After he responded, he went into his contacts and changed AVOID to JADEN. That's the way it should be.

"Hi, Papi!"

At the sound of her voice he dropped the phone like it was on fire. He wasn't even sure he'd finished updating Jaden's information. When he looked up, his eyes came to rest on near perfection. Irena, clad in a blue dress, leaned in the window with her cleavage practically spilling into the front seat. Her eyes sparkled like always.

"Ay! Hey, girl. You scared me." He stuttered as he struggled to retrieve his phone from the floorboard.

"Really? I didn't think I had that effect on you." She laughed, but her eyes never left his. "Not any more anyway. But I remember a long time ago…" She stood, leaving him staring at her stomach.

"Oh, shit! Sorry. Let me get the door." He nearly broke his leg trying to get out of the car and stopped dead in his tracks upon seeing a mountain of a man standing behind her.

"Don't worry, sir. I'll get it for her."

Irena smiled at the gorilla and rolled her eyes at Ivan.

"Fair enough, boss." He spun himself back into the car. Once her door shut, Irena leaned over and kissed him on the cheek. "Thanks for coming out tonight. It's great to see you."

He could feel the heated imprint of her lips on his cheek. "It's my pleasure, girl. Good to see you too. Damn, you are all done up! Am I underdressed? You said small and casual right?"

"Oh, you're fine. You look great, and I have to say the beard is… it's very sexy. You never wore a beard when we were together."

"Well, I don't know if I was ready for a beard back then," he said with a bit of a giggle. "I'm a big boy now."

She sighed. "You and your jokes. How I've missed them."

Dammit. What is this? Flirting? Friendly? What? Just laugh. "Hahaha. So what do you feel like? Sushi? Italian? Greek?"

"Actually, there's a great little restaurant I'd like to try out. I have some friends meeting us there."

"Irena, this sounds a bit more than casual." He looked at her with one eyebrow raised. "This sounds planned — organized and reserved in advance."

"What? It's just a few friends. You're dressed fine. Don't worry."

"Ay, ay, ay. You and your mystery. I'm not sure I miss that."

She dropped her jaw and smacked him on the shoulder. "Papi!"

"Just a joke." He laughed and let the spontaneity of the moment ride, then found himself patting her bare knee. He pulled his hand back.

Her open-jawed gaze turned to a playful smile. "I know you were. You're too easy."

Beep-beep! A valet in the car behind them glared through the window. Shifting Candy into gear, he accelerated out of the alley and toward an unknown venue.

Irena flipped on the music and Dave Matthews came blaring through the speakers. She shot a look of surprise at him, followed by a sly smile.

Ivan played it cool. "What? He's still one of my favorites. That didn't change." He matched her sly smile with a wink and a cocky grin.

"Me too." Her smile faded, and she continued to stare at him as he drove.

Approaching an intersection, Ivan inquired, "Heading?"

"Take a left. We're going to a restaurant called Bianca."

Nerves bounded through him. "Why? Why are we going there?" *Agh.* He silently cursed himself and his growing queasiness. He sounded frantic.

She looked sideways at him. "Because that's where they suggested we go. Not good?"

"*They* chose?"

"Yes. Is there a problem?"

"No, no. I'm just surprised. They have great food, and on a weekend I'll be surprised if we can get a table without a reservation."

Fuck! Okay, relax and breathe. Coincidence is a son of a bitch sometimes, and it was one hell of a son of a bitch tonight. Jaden no longer worked there, so it wasn't a catastrophe, he reminded himself. Worst case scenario is that she finds out through the grapevine he was there with Irena and gets pissed. Best case scenario? Fuck it, there wasn't one.

"Don't worry about a reservation," Irena said. "Let's not worry about anything tonight and have some fun. Please? I need some fun!"

"Fun."

"Yes, fun! You remember how to have fun, don't you, Papi?"

"Yes, I'm looking forward to it," he said, willing his minor panic attack away. "You know we could've walked. It's only a few blocks."

Pointing down at her heels she looked at him as if he were nuts. "Really, Ivan?"

They shared a good laugh, and he felt her hand come to rest on his thigh. "Ah, yes. High society now."

Digging her fingers into his leg she reminded him, "I can still kick your ass, though."

Again they laughed. Thankfully the restaurant appeared right in front of them, because he was about to either say something stupid or get hard. And he didn't want to do either just now. *You are still mad at her, Ivan! Remember that.* He forced the lustful feelings aside and encouraged friendly ones to take the lead.

He pulled Candy up to the valet, jumped out, and tore around to open her door. The doormen looked confused as he helped the starlet to the entrance. He felt a rush — of both adrenaline and fear — as he opened the door under their scrutiny. *Thank God there are no cameras.*

She smiled as she breezed past him and whispered, "Let's have fun tonight, Ivan."

You are still mad at her!! Ivan watched Irena's hips sway in front of him as she floated into the restaurant, and he felt an eagerness flush through his body. It clearly remembered her. They'd done this so many times before, but as lovers not friends. The fact that he was staunchly in the friend zone for the moment was inconsequential. Friends or lovers, being in Irena's orbit scared him.

She glanced over her shoulder and shot him a smile as she reached for his hand. She pulled him up next to her and held on to his hand for a second too long, as if making her intentions known. "Come on! You're getting slow in your old age."

"Slow! I'm pretty sure you're the elder by a few months, young lady."

She shot him a cock-eyed glance. "Same tired joke, still?"

"Same tired girl."

Irena's mouth fell open in a fake gasp and she stopped walking.

"I'm kidding, babe. I see you still haven't developed much of a sense of humor, though." He slid his fingers over her hips and took note of the firm, slender muscles that wrapped around them. His gaze fell into hers as the force field he'd put up had a brief lapse in power. It wavered for a second as a timeless game of "what if we" filled the space between her body and his.

"Ivan, I didn't know you'd be here!" A baritone voice interrupted them.

He disengaged from the staring contest and looked past Irena to see Geoff standing with an awkward look plastered across his face — a look Ivan was certain his face mirrored as Irena turned to see who had interrupted their moment.

"I didn't know you were coming tonight," Geoff repeated.

"Me either," Ivan responded as he turned to Irena.

"Surprise!" she said.

"Geoff, this is—"

"Ms. Stang," he finished. "I'm a big fan and so honored you elected to join us this evening."

"My pleasure. I hear the food is fantastic."

The two men shared a discombobulated look as Geoff motioned to the dining area.

"Yes, well, tonight it…ah…Thank you so much. Your party is this way. Thank you again, Ms. Stang."

Geoff turned and seemed to be wishing to disappear as quickly as possible. He bumped into a server and nearly knocked over a chair as he went.

Ivan couldn't help but snicker and sigh. The poor guy seemed as nervous about all this as he was. "Interesting."

"What was that about?" Irena asked.

"No clue. That's a first. He's generally a pretty calm and cool guy. I've never seen him that scattered."

"Hmm…"

He shrugged, and they headed in to the private party. He watched as a velvet rope was lifted and the security guards and attendants moved aside to allow them unchecked passage.

"Just like old times," she whispered as she snaked her arm around his, letting her breast skim across his arm.

His body trembled with guilt as he had no chance to avoid the contact or the appearance it would give as they entered the room. *Fuck it.* He gave in to his role as escort as he and Irena entered the beautifully decorated space. As if someone had flipped a switch, the music faded and the crowd of twenty or so people craned their necks.

Ivan felt Irena nestle against him as she began to make her rounds. As they circled the room, she made sure to introduce him to everyone she came in contact with, from fellow actors to producers to investors.

"Is this the guy you were telling us about, Irena?" The plumped lips of an overpriced trophy wife well past her prime circled around her words.

Ivan turned and gave Irena an inquisitive look. He wondered who else she might have been talking to about him.

Without missing a beat, Irena snuggled into his side and smiled. "Yes, it is."

"Ah, the doctor. The sex doctor."

"Sex doctor? Irena, I'm very curious what you've been telling these people." He laughed, looked back and forth between the stranger and Irena, and took a step back. "Actually, ma'am, I'm a pediatrician."

An embarrassed Irena and mortified woman stared at each other as Ivan burst into laughter. After another shocked moment they joined him.

"I'm just teasing," he finally added. "Yes, ma'am, I do have a sexual enhancement specialty as part of my medical practice. I'm Ivan. It's nice to meet you."

They continued their mingling as numerous waiters with trays of chargrilled oysters and bruschetta swished through the crowd, as did servers bearing pomegranate martinis. Martini after martini passed Ivan's lips, and the conversation and networking looked and sounded as it had years before when he and Irena had worked a room in tandem. It was a dance they knew well. He had to stop and relish the beauty of it. She'd risen to the top of the world, yet hadn't changed at all when it came to working a room.

"Could everyone take their seats, please? We're going to begin dinner service," Geoff announced.

Without warning, Irena grabbed his arm and tugged him to their seats, which were, of course, front and center.

Ivan shuffled around her and made sure to pull her chair out and tuck her in to the table before taking his seat. And, of course, the trophy wife made sure to sit next to him and continue her discussion about sexual health.

The army of waiters that had been serving various drinks and appetizers now papered the tabletops around the room with menus.

"Here you go, Dr. Rusilko." A familiar face from the wait staff smiled next to him as he handed him a menu.

"Everything good with you?" Ivan asked.

"Yes, it is. Thank you for asking. Enjoy your meal." The man ogled Irena for a moment and gave him one final questioning glance before he continued his duties.

"Are you a regular here?" Irena asked, cocking her head and grinning.

"No. Not now. I used to be." He prayed his answer sounded less awkward than it seemed.

"Hmmm…" she said. Then she changed the subject. "So what are you going to have for dinner?"

"Well, it's apparently a libido-boosting menu," he said, feeling awkward all over again.

"Right up your alley, isn't it?" The trophy wife inserted herself again into the conversation.

"Hmm, let's see here." He chuckled, humoring her. He focused his now slightly inebriated attention on the menu before him.

Ivan began to sweat as his stomach turned over not once, but twice. "Well?"

As he snapped back to a shitty reality he murmured, "Umm… grilled asparagus and lemon."

"That's it?"

"Yeah. Not very hungry."

Leaning over, Irena whispered, "Are you okay, Papi? You look upset all of a sudden." She placed her hand on his leg, letting her fingers pass intimately along his inner thigh as she inquired.

Now fearing that at any moment Jaden might turn the corner or pop up out of nowhere, he assured her he was fine and adjusted in his seat so she had no choice but to remove her hand. Where the freak would have roared to life a few weeks ago, he now heard only a breathless, begging voice inside his head. *God, let's get out of here.*

CHAPTER 29

"One"

$\mathscr{J}$aden had plated the first appetizers so the team would be sure of her desired presentation, and as they'd made their way back to the kitchen with empty trays, she'd been pleased to hear the early reviews from the dining room were raves. She was back on her game.

Now that it was time for the entrées, she was in the zone. She'd always believed food made with love and passion tasted better than any perfectly executed dish prepared without it. Recipes were the road maps, and technique dictated the journey, but when sheer joy entered the mix, flavor and beauty collided to create the most delectable bites. So she'd pushed aside all her questions, all her hurt and frustration about how this dinner had come to be, and thrown herself into the act of feeding people — to creating beauty that also sustained. There was no room in her kitchen for Irena.

"Fire twelve tuna, six hens, and seven vegetarian!" Jaden shouted through the service window at the line cooks.

"How many veg, chef?"

"Seven!"

"Thank you, chef!"

"I also need six more burratta fig apps for late arrivals, please!"

"Six fig, chef. Right away, chef."

"Thank you!"

She loved the rhythm and madness of the kitchen. There was nothing like the noise, the chaos, and the control and power she wielded when she was in charge. She missed this—the messiness, the frenetic energy, and the raw sense of accomplishment.

Once she'd guided the staff through dinner—and grown dizzy watching the sommelier bring out bottle after bottle of wine for the apparently very thirsty crowd—all that remained was dessert.

"These doughnuts will need to be made fresh for every order. I want them crispy, not greasy, got it?"

The guys on the line nodded as she painstakingly plated the playful presentation, topping it with a dusting of nutmeg before leaving her staff to it. She then set off to consult with her pastry chef. The cake created to celebrate the production was gorgeous, and no doubt tasted just as good, but with it came a shit show she dreaded.

She cringed inside when Geoff pushed into the kitchen and approached her. "They're asking for you, darling."

"Excellent!" She ran her hand over her head and tugged off her cap.

She'd been lost in her love for this work for hours, so there was no reason to panic now. Irena was only unpleasant if she gave her the power to be. And anyway, if Irena had been hoping she'd fail, she was likely quite disappointed by now. This was *her* house, and Irena was a guest. A good hostess would go out and greet her guests. Jaden was nothing if not a good hostess, as well as a bad-ass rock star chef who'd just delivered the meal of her career, if she did say so herself. Her body hummed with energy and a confidence she hadn't felt in months.

"Just give me ten to freshen up, and I'll be ready to trot out there like a good little network whore should." She smiled, but Geoff did not.

"Jaden! You are nobody's whore!" he said with enough indignation and venom that she couldn't hide her laughter.

She hugged him. "I appreciate it, Geoff, but I think Kevin might disagree with you."

"I'm serious, Jaden," he continued, still resolute. "No one...I should tell—"

"I know, Geoff. I know." She patted his chest and turned toward the break room, wondering why he followed her as she unbuttoned her not-so-pristine jacket and went inside. He was still talking, but she wasn't listening. He was sweet to be so fierce about her, but this had to be done—and for herself, not the network. But delivering that goddamn cake was the final hoop she'd be jumping through for anyone this evening.

She released her hair, brushed it, and re-gathered it into a sleek ponytail. She blotted a tissue over her face and freshened her makeup. She tossed her jacket and packed up her knives so she'd be clear to make a quick exit after she'd done her job. She slipped on a clean, crisp, high-neck white jacket and buttoned up. But she did change back in to her sky-high Louboutins.

You kicked ass, she told the self she saw in the mirror. *You're gonna kick ass tomorrow and the day after that and the day after that. Irena doesn't matter. You did exactly what you wanted to do here. You should be proud.* She managed a lopsided smile at her reflection. It fell a little short of the Stuart Smalley-style soliloquy she was going for, but at this point she was way past *I'm smart, I deserve good things, and dammit, people like me.* It didn't matter anymore if people liked her. She had to like herself. And she knew now she would get there. She brushed her hands down the front of her jacket and took a deep breath.

She'd prolonged the inevitable as long as possible. She had sparklers to light, a cake to present, and one last dragon to slay before she could crawl into bed and give in to the exhaustion and emotion of the day.

"That tuna was exquisite," remarked a funny little round fellow. He looked almost sad as the waiter cleared his plate away.

Based on the little man's proximity to the woman who'd been chatting with him about sexual health all night, Ivan assumed he was the man who bankrolled the trophy that sat between them. He had to concur with the gentleman's assessment. The tuna was superb. Jaden had mastered its simple perfection. Had it really been less than two years ago when he'd first tasted it at Bianca? Lately it seemed like he'd lived but a moment with her and a lifetime without her already.

What if she came out and caught him with Irena? Well, not caught him, but saw him with his ex. Was he a bad person for being here? Was he bad wherever here was? No. Life goes on. He'd told her as much. They weren't together, so he wasn't in the wrong, and he shouldn't feel guilty. It was a coincidence. That's all.

But he still felt unsettled. Maybe he could slip out to the restroom. Surely now, at the end of dinner, was most likely when she'd come out to say hello. *Or I could fake a very important phone call.* A call from a patient would be a perfect escape from this impossible, uncontrollable situation. He patted his pockets, searching for his phone.

"So how long have you two been together?" the trophy wife's husband asked, motioning between Ivan and Irena.

"Wha-wha-what?" Ivan could only stutter out a question as he felt Irena's hand on his thigh again.

"Well, unfortunately we aren't together anymore," she said. She squeezed his thigh tighter and smiled sadly, looking down at her plate.

Unfortunately! What? His mind's metabolism had kicked up to a sprinter's pace, and he was growing exhausted. He circled and chased his thoughts between worrying about hurting Jaden's feelings, trying to sort out whether he was here as Irena's friend or her date, and hoping to understand what the hell it was that he wanted in life and love. He dug his fingers into his other thigh and forced himself to focus. To be in the moment.

"Yes, those were the days, weren't they?" He smiled back at her and placed his hand on her thigh. When she met his eyes he squeezed tenderly. Her smile changed imperceptibly, and she stared at him as if he'd just granted some unspoken permission.

"Ah, I see," the man said, still eyeing them. "So how did you meet?"

"Business actually," Ivan responded. "I was in town doing some work and was introduced to her through a mutual acquaintance. The rest, as they say, was history."

"Well, you seem very happy in each other's company for a couple that's not together," his wife blurted, escalating the situation from semi-uncomfortable to full-on awkward.

"Well…" Irena began.

The sound of metal clinking against glass filled the room as a man of clear importance stood to speak.

Damnit! There was no way Ivan could sneak out now. He was trapped—a prisoner to impending guilt and embarrassment. He felt

Irena's grip on his thigh slide more inner and upper than propriety would tolerate, and almost far enough that lust could appreciate.

"Ladies and gentlemen, thank you for coming out tonight to celebrate the kick-off of what's sure to be a fantastic shoot here in the sexiest city in the world. And we want to thank Bianca for hosting such an amazing event."

He paused, as did Ivan's beating heart. He knew what the next words out of the guy's mouth were going to be.

"And, of course, we want to thank our special chef for the night, Ms. Jaden Thorne, who we were lucky enough to coerce into this kitchen during her hiatus from *One Hot Kitchen*. She cooked us an amazing, sexy dinner tonight, didn't she?"

As he finished his sentence, applause erupted around the room, and Jaden appeared with the most gracious of smiles. She looked confident and impeccably polished—as it if hadn't been hot in the kitchen at all. A cold sweat washed over him, just as it had when he read her name on the menu, and he was bathed again in anxiety and uncertainty.

He shifted in his seat, trying to remove Irena's hand from his leg. Not because he didn't want it there, he told himself, but because it was inappropriate considering the circumstances. But this time his wiggling didn't work, and her fingers remained in place.

He was torn between looking at Jaden or waiting for her to find him or just looking away in guilt. No, he had to look.

As she made her way around the neighboring tables, shaking hands and meeting people, he wondered what was to come. A fight? A scene? Tears? He trembled at the thought of it and shrank farther into his seat as she came closer and closer.

As one of the producers finally brought her to his table, the feelings inside him threatened to split him in two. He could never have imagined that the two women who'd defined and shaped his beliefs about love—and made him the man he was in the process—would end up in the same room at the same time. With him in the middle.

"And I'm sure Irena needs no introduction," the producer told Jaden as she turned to greet her and instead crashed into his anxiously awaiting gaze.

He watched as her surprise morphed into anger, which evolved into embarrassment and dissipated into sorrow, only to fade away to nothing but a pair of green eyes looking back through him.

Irena released her grip on his thigh to stand and greet Jaden. He followed her to his feet, never looking away from Jaden, though she'd shifted her attention to Irena as if he didn't even exist.

"I enjoyed the dinner, Ms. Thorne. It was delicious. Thank you so much."

Jaden extended her hand and thanked Irena.

"And this is—" Irena continued.

"Hello, Dr. Rusilko. Nice to see you again. I hope you enjoyed the dinner as well?"

As the producer and Irena faded to black, Ivan faced a woman—not a lover or his baby girl—just a self-possessed woman who had her hand outstretched to say hello and thank you for coming to dinner. That was it. No tears, no flying fur, and definitely no blow up. Just hello.

A revelation washed over him as he reached out and shook her hand, nodding as a man solidifying a truce: She was over it. She was over him, and she was gone. Her eyes were silent, foreign, and carrying none of the vibrancy that used to speak to him without saying a word. Now, in the heavy silence that hung between them, they didn't say anything at all.

"Well, I'm very happy you all enjoyed your meal. Please let us know if there's anything else you need this evening."

"Maybe two more pomegranate martinis? You liked those, right, Papi?" Irena bumped him with her shoulder.

Not giving Ivan the chance to formulate a response, Jaden jumped in. "I'll be sure to get you both drinks right away." She took one last look at Ivan, smiled, and returned to the kitchen.

"Wow, is she gorgeous," their table companion noted, staring at her high-heeled legs as they strode away. "I wouldn't mind waking up to that every morning. She could cook me an omelet!"

"Andrew!" his wife responded.

"What? It was a joke." He shot Ivan a glance and waggled his eyebrows.

Ivan managed a weak smile as he sat back down. He knew all too well how amazing that was. Relief flooded his body now that the moment of confrontation had passed—and without any sort of confrontation. His months of struggle over Jaden now seemed resolved, but was this what he wanted? For the first time he had no control over the situation. He'd always had the option to pick up the phone and answer one of the hundreds of texts and calls and emails Jaden had sent after the split. And even after their conversation on the beach, he believed deep down that he had set the terms of their moving forward and probably still had the ability to adjust their status with a simple call. But now? Now she was gone. He wondered if he'd have any place in her life at all. He was free of the consequences and guilt of not letting her back into his life, but he was also stripped of any remaining connection to something he had loved so irrevocably.

Before he could do any additional deciphering of the last few minutes, he felt a delicate hand glide across his thigh for a third time — in a way that would have made the freak rejoice at the intention it carried.

Irena tossed back the last bit of her drink and slid even closer to him. "I don't need another martini. Wanna get out of here? Maybe go back to your place for a nightcap?"

Lust burst through his mind, ready to do battle with any hint of uncertainty he might have about taking her up on her offer. He was powerless now to pick up the phone and make it right with Jaden. He was single and unattached. Did he want to be? He had no fucking clue. But was he going to see if *this* was right? Goddamn right he was. What did he have to lose?

Slamming back the last swig of fruit-flavored liqueur, Ivan looked in her eyes, down at her hand on his, and then back at her. "Sounds good, Mami."

CHAPTER 30

"Breathe Me"

*A*s he fumbled with his keys, Ivan glanced at Irena, who stood next to him in the hallway, smiling as he struggled. She held her purse just in front of her slender torso with her hands crossed over it. Her hair had begun to escape from the tight bun on top of her head, and strands now fell around the sides of her face. She looked a bit feline, and very sexual. He could feel himself going a little wild at the thought of it.

Finally he swung the door of his apartment open, and the darkness of the unknown greeted them. Stepping aside, he allowed her to walk through the door and become the first woman to enter his apartment since he'd moved in — well, other than the housekeeper and his mother. And as he'd established, his recent interest in a maid service now seemed to have been in foresight of this exact moment. He had to admit that he saw this coming, and as much as he wanted to deny it, he couldn't.

She gave him a meaningful look as she slid past him, her eyes exuding excitement and entitlement. He felt himself grow hard as thoughts of naughty nurses and public sexual explorations, along with the rest of their hot history, passed in his mind's eye. He dropped his head back and blinked up at the ceiling, allowing himself one last chance, one last instant to change the plan before he closed the door behind him and officially let Irena in.

Click. The sound of the door sliding into place was almost unnerving.

A lamp illuminated the spacious apartment, and Irena headed for the stereo, which pleaded to be used. She took her phone out of her little bag and made quick work of connecting it to the electronic system. She spun around just as the opening riff of Dave Matthews' "Stay or Leave" began to hum through the speakers.

He marveled at how familiar she seemed—her body, her movements. She hadn't changed since the night they'd parted ways so bitterly. His recollection of that night—elevator doors closing in front of a face he'd so adored and stripping him of his very identity—had for years played on a loop in his mind during tough times. But now that same face looked at him seductively as she moved closer and closer to him with a swagger that drove him insane. She could still seduce him with a bat of her eyelashes or a flick of her pinky finger.

When she settled in front of him, though he was still frozen near the front door, she slipped her hands over his chest, across his shoulders, and around his neck leaving him paralyzed with the realization that this was real, and it was relevant. As each note lifted and each beat drifted, Irena's hips began to sway, tantalizing and tempting him to make his past his present and take her in a way only he knew how.

Back and forth their bodies rocked as they stared into each other's eyes. *What is this?* They floated across the floor, lost in a romance that had been packed away and put on ice for years. *Is this right?* He asked himself, his conscience, his heart, and his soul, but none of them had an answer. Apparently even the freak had gone deaf, dumb, and blind.

As the verse in the song approached that defined their once-passionate love, Irena's eyes searched his, asking for acceptance, a welcome back into a life she had forfeited. Crumbling under the idea of a destiny that had gone unfulfilled, he closed his eyes and gave in to her gentle pull. He dropped his chin and tentatively kissed her. But careful and cautious quickly turned to greedy as she parted his lips to indulge in a bit of forbidden fruit. In that moment he needed to taste her mouth and verify it was as sweet as he remembered. Yes, her taste was still a mystical addiction.

Yet *what if* still stood before him—even as her arms wrapped around his neck and her lips pressed against his. The questions ate away at him in a torrent of *is this right?* and *what the fuck?*

Though his heart remained concerned with protecting himself—again—his hand floated down across the small of her back and came to rest on the curve of her ass. His fingers dug in, forcing her pelvis into his growing excitement. She exhaled against him and grabbed the back of his hair, ripping his head back in a lustful fury.

He forced his head forward again, against the painful pulling, to look her in the eyes, in the soul, and establish that he was the dominant one, not her. She'd played her games long enough. He felt her acquiesce, and he relished the feeling of control. He did not like when it was absent.

"God, I've missed this," she gasped as her hands released his hair and cupped his jaw.

His heart rate quickened, and his mind relinquished the last barrier that stood between them and a night of carnal remembrance. Placing one foot behind the other, he began to back into the bedroom and toward a decision he felt he was ready for.

Their lips left little space between them as their passion mounted. The bedroom was dark and cold, but the heat between the once-again lovers generated a fire. Standing before the bed, he grasped her face and in the hallway light was captivated one last time by the shimmer in her clear, aquamarine eyes. Crushing his lips to hers, he teased her with his tongue, savoring everything familiar and sweet about this woman he'd once known better than he'd known himself.

Irena returned his passion, grasping his shoulders and forcing him down onto the bed. She stepped back for a moment to free her body from her blue dress, and he marveled at the way her nipples stood taut in the dim, shadowy light.

Wearing only a thong, she crawled on top of him, covering him with her body and blanketing him with her presence. His dick pleaded for redemption, but his heart reminded him of his father's words. *What's the one thing you can't find in anyone else?*

Irena raised her arms and loosened the pins that secured her hair, letting it all fall around her face in a glorious tangle of sexuality and vigor. She leaned forward, resting her hands on his chest and pressing him further into the abyss.

Ivan just lay there, looking up at the girl who'd introduced him to love, as well as the definition of heartbreak. She was draped over him in nothing but a thong. The girl he'd come within a hair's breadth of asking to be his one and only. *Just six months ago Jaden was The One... You were sure of it.*

Every sensation within him said yes except for one.

CHAPTER 31

"Chasing Cars"

He stared at the ceiling for another moment before he knew he'd fucked up.

Everything was there: her looks, taste, feel, and even the idea of her, but he was missing what he needed to be complete: the scent of passion, of long nights lost in a lover's gaze only to be followed by a morning of losing his breath, of drowning in the sensation and smell of his true love's neck as he held her tight and knew who he was.

Irena had everything going for her, except that. That perfume of brilliance and sustainability was what he needed, and it wasn't here. The only person who did have it, he'd tossed aside on a blind tear, a self-pitying scorched-earth policy that let him hide behind betrayal, but, as the ultimate punch to the gut, may have cost him eternal happiness. He needed that scent, that embrace, and he couldn't live or love without it. And he was going to reclaim it. *Now.*

He sat up, forcing Irena up along with him, though she remained wrapped around him. Pulling her lips from his neck, he looked into her eyes, finally confident that the decision he was about to make was the right one.

"Irena, you will always be a part of me, but this isn't working."

"Really?" She pressed herself against his firm cock. "I think it's working just fine."

"It's not you, Irena. Please understand that."

"It's her…" Her voice was soft, but not at all surprised.

He looked at her for the first time in his entire life as a friend and nodded.

"Then run to her. She's a lucky girl."

Ivan blinked back at her, shocked by her selfless response. She released him and slipped off his lap.

"Don't get lost in the details, Ivan. You always get lost in planning your life, instead of living your life."

"What did you say?"

"Don't plan to love, Ivan. Go do it. Live! Doesn't matter if it's what you expected or the way you had it all worked out." She suddenly seemed like a gloriously wise, beautiful — albeit nearly naked — oracle. "You plan too much. You're so careful."

Ivan held her face and studied her one last time. He was thankful she'd been the one to shape his heart and was now the one to reveal the missing piece that would make him whole again. He pressed a quick kiss to her forehead. "I don't know how to tell you how thankful I am for you. Thank you so much, Irena."

He shot out of the bed, grabbed his clothes, and then remembered to ask, "Will you be okay getting home?"

"Of course," she assured him, making a "run along" motion with her hands.

So he did. He ran toward the girl who had that one thing no one else had. Out the door he went — his dick still rock hard from a night of close encounters — down the stairs, and out the lobby doors.

Moments later he crested the adjacent lobby entrance, but didn't waste time signing documents or checking in. However, when he bolted past the half-asleep security guard, he forfeited the luxury of an elevator and instead ran up the twelve floors, but he hardly noticed. His heart was driving a body that was fueled by a dream. Adrenaline was just a word. Passion was his fuel.

Bursting through the stairwell door, he finally came face to face with 1218. The last time he'd stood here he'd been a coward, too proud to understand his role in the devastation — too busy working his plan and following his rules to see how wrong he'd been. This time he was here to throw himself at the feet of the woman who held his heart and his happiness, who soothed his soul and made his spirit dance. He would beg for forgiveness.

Inhaling deeply then blowing it all out in one cleansing breath, he swallowed his pride and hesitation and knocked with everything he had.

Boom. Boom. Boom. The two o'clock in the morning barrage most likely woke half of the residents on the floor, but he didn't care. He had one thing on his mind. To make them right. He listened until he could hear her shuffling to the door.

"Ivan, what do you need?"

Fear jolted him as he realized she wouldn't even open the door, but he would plead his case. He pressed his hands flat against the metal and leaned his cheek against the cold barrier that kept him from her. "Jaden, I need to talk you."

"It's late. Can we talk some other time? I'm changed and ready for bed."

Dropping his head, he willed himself not to panic, not to lose it. He closed his eyes, pressed his forehead against the door, and offered a deal. "If I can guess what you're wearing will you open the door?"

She sighed, but after a moment she agreed.

"Hair in a ponytail, no makeup, mismatched socks, some sort of ridiculous T-shirt with an anime cat or some god-awful pattern on it, and a pair of black yoga pants you only threw on to cover up the thong you were sleeping in."

Another extended pause finally ended with the sound of a bolt unlocking and the doorknob turning. He had guessed correctly. The door creaked open and a goddess with a messy ponytail appeared. She was perfection. Sure enough she wore one blue and one yellow sock, black pants, and a bad green T-shirt that hung two sizes too big on her small frame. He also noticed that her eyes were puffy and her skin blotchy and red. Either she'd gone two rounds with Evander Holyfield, or she'd been crying.

Clearly trying to hide her appearance, she reached up and pulled out her hair tie, freeing all that gorgeous dark hair to fall around her face and shoulders. She avoided eye contact, which nearly brought him to his knees. His breath hitched at the thought of being turned away and never again calling her his one and only.

"Baby girl," he breathed.

She looked up, but what he saw in her face and in her green eyes leveled him. He dropped his head reverently and spoke from his heart.

"I'm so sorry. Sorry for what happened to us. It wasn't your fault, it was mine." He watched as she readjusted her feet. "I did this."

"Ivan, I—"

"We didn't need a storybook engagement," he continued. "I just thought we did. We didn't need an Italian serenade. I just thought we did. I couldn't have been more wrong. What we needed was just each other, and I couldn't see that. My being gone, my being busy, all the focus on my business, no matter how well-intended it may have been…I thought I was building a life for us, but that was *me* pulling the trigger on what we could have been. Not you."

He dared raise his head to look at her for a moment, still scared he might have lost his miracle forever. She remained standing there, so he kept going.

"And I'm sorry for letting you shoulder the weight of a tragedy I created. I'm sorry I shut you out instead of listening. I'm sorry I was so afraid. But I know now that you are the reason God put me on this earth. You're the drive behind my next breath and the force between each beat of my heart. You make me smile in a way that defies anatomy. The touch of your skin, the taste of you on my lips, the way you look at me and I can see the man I want to be reflected in your eyes—Jesus, Jaden, even your smell overwhelms me. But more important than any of that, you loved me more than I could understand, without reservation and despite the flaws I was too blind to see, and that's what excites me the most about you. Love without reason is true love, and that's what we have."

He met her eyes as he made his final plea. "I'll go wherever, do whatever, and be whoever you need to remind you how we once were and where we were going. I'm terrified to think of a life where I don't wake up next to you, more in love in the morning than when we went to sleep the night before. I caused this, and I want to fix it. I need to fix it. I am sorry."

He watched as life returned to the most beautiful eyes he'd ever seen. It was her again, not just a woman standing before him. She seemed confused and looking for the right words, but finally she just smiled, and her eyes filled with tears.

"I'm sorry too," she said.

He nodded and cursed quietly as his own vision blurred. He felt a single tear slip down his cheek. Then the magnetic force of the passion in the moment drew him into her arms and their bodies crushed together, their hearts beating frantically against each other's chests. That *one thing* engulfed him as he buried his face in her neck and breathed her in as if it were the first time.

"I love you, Jaden."

"I love you, Ivan."

He took back what he so desperately needed, the lips of the woman he wanted to spend the rest of his life with. He tasted true destiny, and it coursed through his veins, forging their bond forever.

The moment overtook Ivan's body, and he grew hard and pressed against her stomach. Though her eyes were still glassy with tears, they also brewed with another emotion, one more powerful than any they'd ever known: true love's lust.

CHAPTER 32

"A Song for You"

Without thought, without inhibition, without boundaries, Ivan scooped up Jaden and lifted her to his chest. Then he carried her across the threshold toward a better tomorrow. His way lit by the far-off, orangey glow from the marina towers, he carried her to her bedroom to claim her once again as his own.

As he walked, she tasted his neck and ran the tip of her nose along his jawline, nuzzling into his beard. When he reached the bed, he gently placed her on top of the down comforter and guided her head to the pillow, cradling her in his hand. Though he couldn't see her in the darkness, the feeling between them was palpable. He knew that the smile he could feel on his own face covered hers as well.

He placed himself on top of her, straddling one of her legs as the other fell open to the side. The scent of her perfume confirmed once again that this was right, and she was it. He traced the side of her temple down to her lips, stopping only to let her kiss his fingertips before he continued down, trailing along a neck that cried to be kissed. Lowering his face to her throat, he devoured her and felt her body tremble in delight.

She began to rock under his weight, grinding into him as her hands played along his spine and worked through his hair. He drew his hand along her shoulder and across her breast, then past her stomach. Finally he slipped it around behind her to grab her ass, pulling her up high and grinding her against him.

She brought her hands to his chest and unbuttoned his shirt as he continued to taste her neck. Ivan paused to remove his shirt as she did the same, then returning to his spot between her legs and against her now-naked chest, relishing the warmth her body provided. Her excitement fueled a fire that was already burning bright.

Sliding her hand around his neck, she gripped it in one hand and grabbed his ass with the other, forcing his concealed cock against her need.

With the sexiest of voices, she brought her lips to his ear and whispered, "I am yours tonight and for the rest of my life. I want you inside me."

The sound of her voice was enough to fragment him completely, and the message it carried was all he needed. Tucking his hands under her waistband he worked her pants and thong down the length of her legs to the floor.

Bringing his fingers to his mouth, he licked them before they found their way to her already wet pussy. He slid his middle finger in, exploring her gently at first but increasing his speed and depth with each moan she let escape from her body. Higher and higher he worked her until he thought she could take no more, and then he slid a second finger in, releasing her into a much-needed orgasm and him from a prison of emptiness and regret. He had found the arms of his true passion.

He removed his fingers as she elegantly transitioned herself from the submissive position to the dominant, forcing him onto his back. She reached down to unzip his pants, and he caught a glimpse of his personal beauty queen in the window light. He still could scarcely believe it. *She is it,* rang in his ears.

She worked his pants down, over his thighs, calves, and feet before tossing them to the floor. Then she settled over him and pressed his erect cock flush against his stomach. Ivan felt the wetness he'd created cover his dick as she worked against him, parting herself to allow her clit to slide up and down his shaft. Her nipples raked across his chest, causing him to stiffen more and more.

He reached up and held her face with both hands. He rubbed his thumbs along her cheeks and nuzzled his nose against hers, their lips only a breath out of reach.

"I wanted to know what love could be, and I found the answer in you. You're everything to me."

"Oh, baby," she whispered back in the darkness before she ghosted a tender kiss over his lips.

Then she gripped his cock and repositioned it between them, surrendering the power of choice and discretion to make the final move, the final physical manifestation of their immortal love, to him.

Ivan lay paralyzed at the gift she had given him—an opportunity to recommit to their life together as one united soul. Just him and just her.

With a newfound understanding of what life is really about, he committed himself to his love with a single upward thrust. It extracted a burst of sensations that couldn't be explained in any lyrics or any poetic words. It was the most perfect love story ever written.

He writhed in pleasure at the feel of Jaden surrounding every inch of him, and her body contorted as well. They both seemed desperate to capture the full potential for sensual bliss. As their bodies rocked back and forth, they became lost in a place no one else could ever find. Forcing his hips high, Ivan pressed his hand against her ass to maximize their connection as Jaden rocked into him more fully and deeply. He sensed her coming close to the edge, but she forced her legs down and pressed her hands against his chest, stopping his motions completely.

"Not yet, baby," she said through ragged breath. "Stay right there. Stay with me. I want to come together."

He trembled from the inside out and began to give her what she wanted. Without withdrawing, he turned her over on her back and brought both hands behind her to secure her body in place. Back and forth, he penetrated her, working himself up to an instant where they'd share that exclusive moment in love's long road.

The feel of her beneath him, breathing, moaning, twisting, and turning coaxed his spine to loosen and his toes to curl. He was so close. But he didn't need to tell her that…she already knew. Lowering her ass to the bed she made sure to give him what she knew he needed to release.

As his strokes blended chords into a song only they knew, the sweet melodies only she could play sang loud and clear between them—the most intense collaboration he'd ever known. With one final thrust he found not just a sexual nirvana, but a heaven where they existed as one. He came hard and full inside her as she rocked herself around him in a shattering, brilliant orgasmic burst of emotion and power.

Seconds felt like hours as their bodies subsided from the landslide of erotic pleasure. Ivan rolled onto his back and brought Jaden with him. She snuggled into his chest and let her legs twist and tangle comfortably with his as he wrapped his arms around her shoulders. He held her hand over his heart, and they lay in the dark, reminiscing about fountains, limos, balconies, mini golf, sea turtles, vineyards, teddy bears, and motorcycles. They recalled Thanksgiving, guns, cabins, airports, mountains, kitchen counters, showers, doctor's consults, and Mollydooker. Then they talked of Betty, chateaus, dinners, parties, beaches, jewelry, flowers, ridiculously oversized costume hearts, and the moment their eyes met for the first time: one magical night in Sarasota.

As the sun began to creep up, it cast rays of illumination over every entangled inch of their bodies. And with the morning light, something else in the room came into view: Jaden's bags, packed and standing against the wall.

"Going somewhere?" Ivan asked.

"Supposed to be."

"But—"

"Looks like I have a plan B," she said with a giggle. She turned her face into his chest and laughed.

"What's so funny?" he said nervously.

"Nothing. There's nothing funny about any of this," she said, laughing even harder. "I have a plan B!"

He wondered if she might have gone a little crazy but couldn't help laughing along with her. They rode out the fits of giggles and nestled back into their sweet embrace. After a few minutes of contented silence, she spoke.

"I'm not running away any more." She twisted in his arms and put both her hands flat on his chest, then rested her chin on them.

His eyes cut over to the pile of luggage in the corner that said otherwise. She followed his gaze and assessed the implications.

"I mean, I guess technically I am. Running away, that is. From my job, probably. From a career I'd have to be an idiot to walk away from, but that I find I don't want, yes. From you, however? No, never again."

Ivan tried not to smile so big, but he couldn't help it. "So should we just carry those bags to my place? You know it's right next door."

"Wait—what?"

"A few months ago I moved to the next building over," he said with a laugh.

Jaden just shook her head, eyes wide. "Well then, for now I guess we should," she said with a giggle. "You don't mind having a roommate, do you?"

He breathed a sigh of relief as a tiny flicker of fear he hadn't realized he was holding on to was finally snuffed out. She'd chosen him. No second guessing. No hindsight. She chose him.

"No, definitely not," he said as he pulled her into his arms and kissed her.

She sighed contentedly and turned, pressing her backside against him. He began working his hands across her side and along her torso to his favorite spot on her entire body. He parted her hair with the intention of kissing, but found something he hadn't expected and never would have imagined.

She tucked her chin and shifted in front of him, offering a better view. Across the back of her neck, just below her hairline, he found a row of tiny letters—a permanent reminder of what it meant to live in the moment.

Smile

Stopping his pressured finger strokes, he thought for a second. "Because it happened?" he breathed into her ear.

Turning to meet his eyes, she responded with words only one who had lived her life could offer. "Because *you* happened."

Acknowledgments

What is Destiny?

Is it a doctrine formulated by aristocrats and philosophers arguing that there is some unseen driving force predicting the outcomes of every minuscule and life altering moment in one's life? Or is it the artistry illustrated by those under-qualified and over-eager to give their future meaning and their ambitions hope?

Is it a declaration by those who refuse to accept that we are alone in this universe, spinning randomly though a matrix of accidental coincidences? Or is it the assumption made by those who concede that there is a divine plan or pre-ordained path for each human being, regardless of their current station?

I think destiny is a bit of a tease…

Its cynical taunts and teases mock those naïve enough to believe in its black jack dealing of inevitable futures. Its evolution from puppy dogs and ice cream to razor blades and broken mirrors characterizes the fickle nature of its sordid underbelly. Those relying on its decisive measures will fracture under its harsh rules. Those embracing the fact that life happens at a million miles a minute will flourish in its random grace.

Destiny has afforded me the most magical memories and unbelievably tragic experiences that have molded and shaped my life into what it is today…beautiful. I fully accept the mirage that destiny promises and the reality it can produce. Without the invisible momentum carried with its sincere fabrication of coming attractions, destiny is the covenant we rely on to get ourselves through the day.

To the destiny I know awaits me, I thank you in advance.

Thank you to…

- My family—Dave, Suessy, Paul, Cat and Patty—for being supportive.
- Everly Drummond for starting this crazy journey and for sparking my addiction to writing.
- The best damn publicist and amazing friend, Micha Stone. ;)
- The Omnific Team for taking a chance on us! CJ Creel, Lisa O'Hara, Elizabeth Harper, Traci Olsen.
- My ROCK STAR editors Jessica Royer Ocken and Kimberly Blythe.
- Amy Brokaw for creating all the covers and Coreen Montagna for the book design.
- The photo shoot crew, John Conroy, Adrianne, Gail, Jessica, and Brandi, for making the vision a reality.
- Julie, Jillian, Kathy and Kristin, thank you for blogging and championing *TWD* from the beginning.
- The Baby Girls for being truly fantastic supporters and friends!

AND

- To all my ex-girlfriends for providing all the magic moments that kept the series groovy.

Don't cry because it's over…smile because it happened.

ABOUT THE AUTHOR

Dr. Ivan Rusilko, DO, CSN, PT, is the Medical Director and co-Founder at the new Club Essentia Wellness Retreat at Delano. He specializes in creating healthy lifestyles that support longevity and improved overall quality of life through medically supervised and customized diagnostic and treatment programs, with an emphasis placed on personal patient attention and follow-up. A certified sports nutritionist, champion bodybuilder, international male fitness model, and former Mr. USA 2008 and 2010, Dr. Ivan graduated from the Lake Erie College of Osteopathic Medicine in 2010 and sits as the national media and public relations expert and spokesperson on diet, exercise and sports nutrition for the American Osteopathic Association (AOA).

Dr. Ivan has been a feature health writer and lifestyle coach for numerous magazines and online publications including *The Washington Times* and *Quarter Life Health*. He is excited to offer a male voice in a predominantly female-authored genre. Always one with a story to tell, he hopes to continue writing, exploring new genres and projects.

He is proud to bring two of his passions, his medical wellness and sexual health background and writing together in this unique project. He hopes that "The Winemaker's Feast Trilogy" will help spark an enthusiasm and ignite liberation among women, inspiring them to celebrate their sensuality and focus on their sexual health in order to achieve a better quality of life.

check out these titles from
OMNIFIC PUBLISHING

←···→ Contemporary Romance ←···→

Boycotts & Barflies and *Trust in Advertising* by Victoria Michaels
Passion Fish by Alison Oburia and Jessica McQuinn
Three Daves by Nicki Elson
Small Town Girl and *Corporate Affair* by Linda Cunningham
Stitches and Scars by Elizabeth A. Vincent
Take the Cake by Sandra Wright
Pieces of Us by Hannah Downing
The Way That You Play It by BJ Thornton
Poughkeepsie by Debra Anastasia
Burning Embers by Hannah Fielding
Cocktails & Dreams by Autumn Markus
Recaptured Dreams and *All-American Girl* by Justine Dell
Once Upon a Second Chance by Marian Vere

←···→ Paranormal Romance ←···→

The Light Series: Seers of Light, Whisper of Light, and Circle of Light
by Jennifer DeLucy
The Hanaford Park Series: Eve of Samhain and *Pleasures Untold* by Lisa Sanchez
Immortal Awakening by KC Randall
Crushed Seraphim and *Bittersweet Seraphim* by Debra Anastasia
The Guardian's Wild Child by Feather Stone
Grave Refrain by Sarah M. Glover
Divinity by Patricia Leever
Blood Vine by Amber Belldene
Divine Temptation by Nicki Elson

←···→ Romantic Suspense ←···→

Whirlwind by Robin DeJarnett
The CONduct Series: With Good Behavior and *Bad Behavior* by Jennifer Lane
Indivisible by Jessica McQuinn
Between the Lies by Alison Oburia

←⋯→Young Adult←⋯→

Shades of Atlantis and *The Ember Series: Ember* and *Iridescent* by Carol Oates
Breaking Point by Jess Bowen
Life, Liberty, and Pursuit by Susan Kaye Quinn
Embrace by Cherie Colyer
Destiny's Fire by Trisha Wolfe
Streamline by Jennifer Lane
Reaping Me Softly by Kate Evangelista

←⋯→Historical Romance←⋯→

Cat O' Nine Tails by Patricia Leever
Burning Embers by Hannah Fielding

←⋯→Erotic Romance←⋯→

Becoming sage by Kasi Alexander
Saving sunni by Kasi & Reggie Alexander
The Winemaker's Dinner: Appetizers & Entrée by Dr. Ivan Rusilko & Everly Drummond
The Winemaker's Dinner: Dessert by Dr. Ivan Rusilko

←⋯→Anthologies and Singles←⋯→

A Valentine Anthology including short stories by Alice Clayton, Jennifer DeLucy, Nicki Elson, Jessica McQuinn, Victoria Michaels, and Alison Oburia

It's Only Kinky the First Time by Kasi Alexander
Learning the Ropes by Kasi & Reggie Alexander
The Winemaker's Dinner: RSVP by Dr. Ivan Rusilko
The Winemaker's Dinner: No Reservations by Everly Drummond
Big Guns by Jessica McQuinn
Concessions by Robin DeJarnett
Starstruck by Lisa Sanchez
New Flame by BJ Thornton
Shackled by Debra Anastasia
Swim Recruit by Jennifer Lane
Sway by Nicki Elson
Full Speed Ahead by Susan Kaye Quinn
The Second Sunrise by Hannah Downing
The Summer Prince by Carol Oates
Whatever it Takes by Sarah M. Glover
Clarity by Patricia Leever
A Christmas Wish by Autumn Markus